THE FOURTH
BEAR HUG

THE FOURTH BEAR HUG

James D. Navratil

Library of Congress Control Number:		2020917015
ISBN:	Hardcover	978-1-6641-2895-8
	Softcover	978-1-6641-2899-6
	eBook	978-1-6641-2894-1

Print information available on the last page.

Rev. date: 09/21/2020

To order additional copies of this book, contact:
Xlibris
844-714-8691
www.Xlibris.com
Orders@Xlibris.com
817688

Contents

Synopsis of *The Bear Hug* by Sylvia Tascher

The Fourth Bear Hug is a continuation of the stories in *The Bear Hug*, *The Final Bear Hug*, and *The Third Bear Hug*. The following is the summary of the first book.

The prologue of *The Bear Hug* begins at the new headquarters of the International Atomic Energy Agency (IAEA) in Vienna, Austria, where Margrit Czermak is copying for a Soviet security service (KGB) agent confidential documents belonging to her husband, Dr. John James Czermak, a world-renowned nuclear scientist and contributor to the development of the neutron bomb. Subsequently, the Russian agent sexually attacks Margrit, and as she is fleeing, her lover, Andrei Pushkin, intervenes and is shot by the agent.

In chapter 3, a red Mercedes-Benz roadster is seen inching its way around the Gurtel (Vienna's outer perimeter street), the driver eyeing the few scantily clad prostitutes who are soliciting their wares despite the heavy snow that had blanketed the city. We then proceed with him to the third district, where a Ukrainian dance ensemble, sponsored by the United Nations' (UN) Russian Club of Art and Literature, had just finished its performance. During the cocktail party that followed, Andrei Pushkin, suspected by the U.S. Central Intelligence Agency (CIA) of being a covert Russian agent, captivated by a woman's melodious laugh, turned to gaze in her direction. He was immediately enraptured by the beautiful, charming Margrit Czermak gracing the arm of Boris Mikhailov, a prominent man with the IAEA, as he steered her in the direction of her husband. Meanwhile, two covert agents of the KGB, huddled in the background, are discussing the instructions received from the Kremlin to elicit from the prominent American scientist his knowledge of the neutron bomb, by whatever means necessary.

A few months later, on Margrit's return flight from London, where she had been attending her stricken brother, she encountered and was consoled by the compassionate Pushkin. In due course, he invited her to dine with him. As her husband's travel had again necessitated his prolonged absence from the city, in a state of extreme loneliness, she accepted Andrei's invitation.

In the interim, both the KGB and the CIA kept the American woman under surveillance, it being the KGB's intention to instigate an illicit relationship and the CIA's to use her to entrap Pushkin.

At the same time, John Czermak was suffering profound personal problems. While he had been employed in the nuclear weapons field in Colorado, his scientific endeavors had demanded first priority. As his present position with the IAEA had created substantial leisure time, he was both angered and dismayed to realize his wife's newly found independence. And being a man of high moral values, it never occurred to him that his wife was to become romantically involved with another man. To compound matters, he had belatedly sought to create an atmosphere of congeniality with his children, only to discover that he had little rapport with them.

With the passing of time, the clandestine liaison between the American and Russian flourished, eventually culminating in Paris and again in the Soviet capitol. However, realizing the futility of their relationship, they had on several occasions unsuccessfully attempted to terminate it. Meanwhile, the KGB, eager to record on film the boudoir events of the couple, applied pressure to Andrei by kidnapping his younger son. Thus, successful in obtaining the desired photographs, they were able to prevail upon Margrit for information relevant to her husband's work at the Colorado nuclear facility. During an assignation, a CIA agent met his death as he was propelled in front of a high-speed subway train. As Margrit had witnessed the event, an attempt was then made to eliminate her as well.

The relationship with her husband continued to deteriorate, and John made good his threats to leave her. Therefore, she beseeched Andrei to abandon his family to share a life with her. But Andrei had undergone a substantial ideological transformation during his affair with Margrit and, as a result, suffered continual agonizing self-debasement. Thus, he eventually took his own life.

Shocked beyond belief by the receipt of her lover's farewell letter, Margrit deliberated between life and death. Her friend, the Austrian Anna Winkler, who minutes before had heard of Andrei's suicide on the midmorning news broadcast, drove frantically to reach Margrit in time. And John, unaware of the morning's bizarre events but certain he wanted his beloved wife at any cost, rushed to make amends to her from the opposite side of the city.

Synopsis of *The Final Bear Hug* by James D. Navratil and Sylvia Tascher

The Final Bear Hug is a continuation of the story in *The Bear Hug*. The story begins with John James Czermak and his wife, Margrit, returning to their home in Arvada, Colorado, after spending almost three years in Vienna, Austria, where John worked for the IAEA. John is a world-renowned nuclear scientist and contributor to the development of the controversial neutron bomb. He returns to the job as manager of Plutonium Chemistry Research and Development at the Rocky Flats Plant (RFP), where parts for nuclear weapons are made. In Vienna, Margrit was romantically involved with Andrei Pushkin, thought by the CIA to be a KGB agent. Realizing the futility of their relationship, Andrei and Margrit had on several occasions unsuccessfully attempted to terminate it. But Andrei suffered continual agonizing self-debasement and eventually left Vienna for Canada after faking his suicide.

Following their return to Colorado, John and Margrit resumed a close, loving relationship that had been damaged in Vienna. About this time, John was recruited by Tim Smith of the CIA since John traveled to conferences around the world and to Vienna and Moscow to have meetings with his Russian coauthors on a series of books they were writing for the IAEA. Following more contacts with his Russian colleagues, John was informed that a background investigation had been conducted by the Department of Energy (DOE) and the Federal Bureau of Investigation (FBI). This investigation resulted in John losing his security clearance.

John was then granted a three-year leave of absence from Rocky Flats management to teach in Australia. Tim continued to keep in contact with John and asked him to visit certain countries and find out if they might be producing nuclear weapons. During his travels, there were several attempts on his life. After his return from his leave of absence in Australia, John started work in California. It was there that Andrei surprisingly contacted Margrit, trying to renew their love affair. Margrit rejected him since she had a good relationship with John and told Andrei she might go with him if she was a divorcée or a widow. This statement prompted Andrei to try and kill John, but instead, he accidentally killed Margrit. Back at his home in Canada, he learned of her death and committed suicide. In his dying breath, he told his son, Alex, that Czermak had shot him.

John wanted to start a new life and left California for a teaching job at Clemson University in South Carolina and even started using his middle name. Andrei's son, Alex, joined James's research group using a different last name. The story concluded during an expedition in Antarctica that the CIA supported to see if one of the Russian crew members was passing nuclear weapons information to a group of Argentinian scientists.

On the expedition, Alex tried to kill James but later found out that James did not kill his father. On the last night of the voyage, he met James at the stern of the ship and made amends to him, which ended by Alex giving James a big bear hug that caused both of them to accidentally fall into the rough and freezing ocean.

Synopsis of *The Third Bear Hug* by James D. Navratil

The Third Bear Hug is a continuation of the stories in *The Bear Hug* and *The Final Bear Hug*. The story begins in the later book with John James Czermak and his wife, Margrit, returning to their home in Arvada, Colorado, after spending almost three years in Vienna, Austria, where John worked for the IAEA. John is a world-renowned nuclear scientist and contributor to the development of the neutron bomb and returns to his job as manager of Plutonium Chemistry Research and Development at the Rocky Flats Plant, near Denver, Colorado, where parts for nuclear weapons are made. In Vienna, Margrit was romantically involved with Andrei Pushkin, thought by the CIA to be a KGB agent. Realizing the futility of their relationship, Andrei and Margrit had on several occasions unsuccessfully attempted to terminate it. But Andrei suffered continual agonizing self-debasement and eventually left Vienna for Canada after faking his suicide.

Following their return to Colorado, John and Margrit resumed a close, loving relationship that had been severely damaged in Vienna. About this time, John was recruited by Tim Smith of the CIA to see if some countries had a secret nuclear weapon program under way. It was easy for John to collect intelligence information for Tim since he traveled to conferences around the world and to Vienna and Moscow to have meetings with his Russian coauthors on a series of books they were writing for the IAEA. Following more contacts with his Russian colleagues, John was informed that a background investigation had been conducted by the DOE and the FBI. This investigation resulted in John losing his security clearance.

John was then granted a three-year leave of absence to teach in Australia. Tim kept in contact with John and requested him to visit certain countries and find out if they might be producing nuclear weapons. During his travels, there were several attempts on his life. After his return from his leave of absence, he started work in California. It was there that Andrei surprisingly contacted Margrit, trying to renew their love affair. Margrit rejected him since she had a good relationship with John and told Andrei she might go with him if she was a divorcée or widow. This statement prompted Andrei to try and kill John, but instead, he accidentally killed Margrit. Upon hearing the news of her death, Andrei committed suicide and told his son, Alex, in his dying breath that Czermak had shot him and wanted Alex to kill John.

Czermak wanted to start a new life and left California for a teaching job at Clemson University in South Carolina and even started using his middle name, James. Andrei's son, Alex, joined James's research group using a different last name. Ying from China also joined his group, and a loving relationship developed between her and John. The story in *The Final Bear Hug* concluded during an expedition in Antarctica that Tim supported to see if one of the Russian crew members was passing nuclear weapon's information to a group of Argentinian scientists.

On the expedition, James and Ying were married by the captain, and Alex tried to kill James but later found out that James did not kill his father. On the last night of the voyage, during a violent rainstorm, Alex met James at the stern of the ship and made amends to him, which ended by Alex giving James a big bear hug that caused both of them to accidentally fall into the rough and freezing ocean.

The story in *The Third Bear Hug* begins on the morning following the violent storm. A man and two ladies discovered James washed up on the shore of Cape Horn. They took him back by fishing boat to Deborah's home on another island. The couple was Deborah's neighbors, and she was a retired medical doctor.

She assisted James in recovering but found out he had amnesia and did not remember anything prior to being washed up on land. Deborah agreed to let James help her around her small farm. Several months later, the two started to travel to different parts of Chile together, and a loving relationship developed. James's memory slowly returned after an accidental meeting with a friend in Peru and returned to Clemson to have a reunion with Ying, family, and friends. The university appointed James as chairman of the Chemistry Department. During this time, Ying got killed in a hit-and-run accident that was meant for James. A week later, another attempt was made on James's life in his university laboratory, but he managed to escape the Molotov cocktail fire.

James was then contacted by CIA Agent Kim Carn, who requested him to go on certain trips to collect intelligence for the CIA. The last technical conference James attended was in Moscow, and he asked Deborah to accompany him. On the trip, they spent a few days in Vienna, where they got married. The Czermaks then went to Moscow so James could attend the conference. On the last night of the meeting, the two were confronted in their hotel room by a man with a gun, who identified himself as Nikolai Pushkin, Andrei's son and Alex's elder brother. Before he shot Deborah and then James, he said, "This is for killing my father and brother." Gravely wounded, James jumped over and gave Nikolai a bear hug, trying to wrestle the gun from him, but it went off, putting a bullet into Nikolai's heart, killing him.

The story concluded with Deborah dying and James recovering. However, Andrei's brother, Alexei, was determined to kill James since he was convinced that James was responsible for the deaths of his brother and two nephews.

Prologue

The main campus of the University of Colorado (CU) is in Boulder and was established in 1876. The first building was Old Main, surrounded at the time by a barren eight hundred acres of land. The first student body was composed of forty-seven pupils. Macky Auditorium was built in 1923 and Norlin Library in 1940. All three structures still stand today, along with at least five dozen other academic, research, and residential buildings, with more being built. Of course, sidewalks connect the buildings. Among most of the buildings are large grass areas lined with flower gardens, bushes, and trees.

There are three other campuses: Denver, Aurora, and Colorado Springs. It is a public research university and the largest in Colorado with more than 36,000 undergraduate and graduate students and about 4,000 faculty. CU is composed of 9 colleges and schools that offer over 150 academic programs. A total of 12 Nobel Laureates and 20 astronauts have been affiliated with the university. The university was ranked forty-fourth among public universities in the United States by *U.S. News and World Report*. The Boulder campus was named by *Travel and Leisure* as one of the most beautiful college campuses in the United States.

The chemistry building sits across the Dalton Trumbo Fountain Court from the University Memorial Center that houses a restaurant, bowling alley, bookstore, conference rooms, and offices of student activities and organizations. The center is located next to Broadway, one of the main streets in Boulder. The four-floor Cristol Chemistry and Biochemistry Building houses most of the chemistry faculty's offices and research laboratories. Master and doctoral students' research works are advised by over thirty professors in all the major fields of chemistry: analytical, atmospheric, biochemistry, environmental, inorganic, organic, and physical.

One of the fourth-floor offices, in the southwest corner of the chemistry building, is shared by a part-time professor, Dr. John James Czermak, and a visiting professor from the Mendeleev Institute of Technology in Moscow, Dr. Lara Medvedev. She is on a sabbatical for a year at CU. The office is spacious, and Czermak's desk sits against the west wall, and Medvedev's desk is next to the opposite wall. The only window in the room is located opposite the door. The view from the window overlooks the water fountain court and the University Memorial Center with the Flatirons in the distance. The Flatirons are five large slanted rock formations of red conglomeratic sandstone along the eastern slope of Green Mountain. The name comes from their resemblance to old-fashioned clothes irons.

One quiet early evening, with only a few faculty and students in the chemistry building, Medvedev pulls out a hunting knife from her briefcase and goes behind her officemate, who is busy working on his computer. She quickly leans over Czermak and starts stabbing him in the chest several times with the knife as she says, "This is for killing three of my relatives."

A dying Czermak cries out, "I thought you loved me?"

"I do, but promised revenge makes me love my three departed relatives more."

Chapter 1
A New Life in Colorado

I

Immediately following the attempt by Andrei Pushkin's brother, Alexei, to kill John, the nurse at the Moscow hospital was successful in using cardiopulmonary resuscitation (CPR) on Czermak. The following day, John was discharged from the hospital, and his good friend Misa took him to the airport, along with his suitcase. He told John, "The police did not have any luck in finding Alexei, but they will continue to search. I tried to arrange for Deborah's body to be returned to Colorado but with no luck. The authorities suggested that she be cremated and have the ashes shipped to you via DHL or UPS."

"That sounds like a good idea. That way, I can take some of the ashes to Chile and have the rest buried in Pendleton and Nederland. Thank you, dear friend, for all you have done for me."

A very distraught Czermak arrives back in South Carolina. A few days later, he has a memorial for Deborah, which includes placing some of Deborah's ashes under the big oak tree in front of his Pendleton home. Of course, he calls Eduardo and informs him of Deborah's death. "Eduardo, I plan to make a trip to see you and Maria as soon as possible and bring some of Deborah's ashes with me to spread some at the farm, at the central park in Puerto Williams, and at the University of Santiago campus. Then we can discuss what to do with her farm. One idea for you to think about is to make her home into a bed-and-breakfast. I know lots of hikers from overseas hike the trail to Caleta Wulais, and staying at her farm would be more convenient for them. Of course, we would need Maria's approval since she would be doing most of the work as a breakfast maker and room cleaner. Or maybe you could hire someone else to take care of hikers that would stay there."

The next morning, John receives a call from Kim Carn, who invites him for lunch. During lunch at the Pendleton Plantation restaurant, Kim tells John that she is so sorry to hear about the death of Deborah. John tells her about his plans to retire and move to Colorado. At the end of the meal, she thanks him for his contributions to the CIA and wishes him good luck in his new life. They go their separate ways after a long hug.

A week later, John attends a goodbye party with his colleagues at Clemson and completes getting ready to move to Colorado, which includes instructing his realtor to sell both his houses. He then starts his three-day drive to Denver in a new Jeep Compass. He had his Smart car shipped to Nederland.

Upon John's arrival in Colorado, he has a reunion with his grown children at Eric and Sylvia's home in South Boulder. John stays at his son's home until the builders, whom he had contracted before his return to Boulder, complete the remodeling of his house in Nederland as well as build a detached three-car garage with a second-story apartment. With John's assistance, the builders work on the house first by converting the three-car garage and large workshop into a living room, two bedrooms with bathrooms, a dining room, and a kitchen with cabinets and appliances, the same floor plan as each of the upper two floors of the house. There was already a laundry room, with washer and dryer, and an enclosed back stairway to the upper two floors that was not changed. The builders continue their construction work, building a detached three-car garage with living quarters on the second floor, identical to each floor in the house. They complete the work after the bathroom fixtures and kitchen cabinets are installed, along with a stove, microwave, and sink. A new refrigerator is also placed in the kitchen, electric heaters are installed in all the rooms, and a beautiful fireplace is constructed in the living room. A washer and dryer are delivered and installed later.

During part of this time, John makes a short visit to Chile to distribute Deborah's ashes in Santiago, in Puerto Williams, and on the farm and have the ownership of her house transferred to Eduardo and Maria. Earlier Eduardo had sent John an e-mail stating that it was not a good idea to use the home as a B and B. He wrote that most of the hikers who went by their home in the past told him that they really liked staying in town with its bars and restaurants. Also, Maria said she would have a hard time taking care of the home and that finding help would be difficult. If Maria and Eduardo sell the property, they agree to give John one-third of the proceeds. However, they all acknowledge it would be difficult to find a buyer. John stays at the home for two more days, enjoying some of Maria's wonderful meals and finishing the legal work. Surprisingly, he finds out that Deborah left him a sizable fortune in cash, gold, jewelry, and stocks. The visit ends with a small memorial at the farm for Deborah that her friends from the city attend.

II

After all the building is completed at John's property in Nederland, which he calls Pine Shadows, the moving van from South Carolina arrives at the home. The movers unload their truck and place the furniture and boxes of household items in the apartment above the garage. Once the boxes are unloaded and furniture arranged, John starts living in the apartment. His renters continue to live in the second and third floors of the house. He plans to rent the first level of the house.

The first Saturday after John starts living in the apartment, he has a housewarming potluck party that his family and friends attend. His longtime friends include a few former West High School classmates and some colleagues whom he worked with at Rocky Flats. After several tours of the apartment and the first floor of the house, everyone enjoys the food. Later, John and most of the guests go to the enclosed covered patio in the back of the garage for several games of pool and ping-pong. A few of the guests play volleyball in the nearby tennis court next to the empty covered swimming pool. After an afternoon of partying and playing games, the visitors and family leave in small groups and return to their homes.

After a wonderful weekend, John visits Bob Stevens, chairman of CU's chemistry department. Bob is a good friend of John and was his postdoctoral advisor decades ago. He thanks John again for inviting him and Betty to the party. Then they reminisce about the good times they had during John's days as a student at CU. After more conversations, Bob offers John a part-time professorship to mainly bring in research money, supervise several graduate students, and present a seminar talk once a semester. John accepts Bob's offer on the condition to only be at the university Mondays, Wednesdays, and Fridays. He tells Bob that he wants to use the other days of the week to complete writing a chemistry textbook, work out at the gym, do some hiking, and when the snow is right, ski at the nearby Eldora ski area. He also plans to learn how to fly a small plane, host visits from neighbors and friends, make some trips around Colorado, and attend conferences in the United States and overseas.

A week after being hired by Bob, John moves into a spacious southwest corner office on the fourth floor of the chemistry building that he will share with a visiting faculty member. His present officemate is a professor from Australia, and he is due to return to the University of Sydney at the end of the fall semester. They have a lot to talk about since John had worked at the University of New South Wales, located in a suburb of Sydney, for three years.

John enjoys a joyous Christmas and New Year with his family. On the second Monday of the new year, Bob brings a beautiful tall blonde, about John's age, to John's office. "John, I would like you to meet Dr. Lara Medvedev a visiting professor from Mendeleev University in Moscow. She is on a sabbatical for a year at CU. I have already showed her around campus and our building and introduced her to most of the faculty and staff."

"Lara, I am so happy to meet you, and welcome to Boulder and the University of Colorado."

"Thank you. I am looking forward to spending a year here and sharing an office with you. Bob and Betty were kind enough to meet me at the Denver International Airport yesterday, take me on a short drive through Downtown Denver and around Boulder, and let me stay at their home in North Boulder until I can find an inexpensive apartment to rent. You can probably guess that Russian faculty are not paid well."

"How would you like to stay in a new apartment at my home in Nederland at no cost? The apartment is in the first floor of my house. A nice family is renting the second and third floors, and I live in an apartment above my three-car garage near the house. However, you would have to buy some furniture, especially a bed unless you want to sleep on the floor. I would ask you to leave the furniture there after you go back to Moscow. You could ride with me to work on Mondays, Wednesdays, and Fridays and take the bus the other two days. You would have to take my second car to the bus stop in Nederland on those two days. Once you reach the main bus station in Boulder, you could walk to campus or transfer to a Boulder bus. An easier option is to just drive my car to campus on nonsnowy days since my Smart car does not do well on icy and snowy roads. Before you say yes or no, let me show you the apartment on Wednesday afternoon."

"John, do you think I should buy a car?"

"I would wait a couple weeks to see if the bus service suits you since cars can be lots of trouble but a convenient way to get around. Of course, I have already offered you the use of Whit."

"Okay, I will take your valuable advice, but I will have to get a Colorado driver's license as soon as possible. Why do you call your car Whit?"

"I like to put names on my houses and cars. I call him Whit since he is painted white. The 'e' is missing."

"John, that is a truly kind and generous offer, so please consider it, Lara. Of course, I told you that you could stay at my home as long as you want, but I can understand how you want to have your own bedroom and living room and a kitchen, where you can make your own meals. By the way, John, I think the name of your red jeep is obvious."

"You are correct, Bob. Lara, please make yourself at home and unpack your suitcase full of books and papers. You can share one of my bookcases. How about the three of us having lunch at the Packer Grill in the memorial center? We will have to watch for ice on the sidewalks. What do you think of all the snow on the ground, Lara?"

"Well, it is warmer here than in Moscow, and of course, we do get lots of snow."

Bob agrees to meet John and Lara in his office at noon.

Over lunch, Bob does most of the talking. "Lara, I would like to tell you more about Denver and Boulder. I think I already told you a lot about CU, and I am sure during your stay, you will learn much more.

"Denver was founded in 1858 and is located in the South Platte River Valley on the western edge of the High Plains, just east of the Front Range of the Rocky Mountains, with an estimated population of almost eight hundred thousand according to *Wikipedia*. It is nicknamed the *Mile-High City* because of its elevation of 5,280 feet above sea level. Snowfall is common from late fall to early spring, and summers can range from warm to hot with occasional afternoon thunderstorms.

"Boulder was founded in 1858 and is located at the base of the foothills of the Rocky Mountains in a basin beneath Flagstaff Mountain. It is twenty-five miles northwest of Denver and has a population of about one hundred thousand. The city is known for its association with gold seekers and being the home of CU. Arapahoe Glacier provides water for the city, along with Boulder Creek, which flows through the center of the city. One of the most popular sections of Boulder is the Pearl Street Mall, home to numerous shops and restaurants. The four-block pedestrian mall is a social hotspot in the city. 'The Hill,' next to the southwest side of campus, is one of the centers of off-campus life for students who mainly hang out at the Sink, a popular bar and restaurant. In fact, the movie star Robert Redford worked there as a waiter during his studies at CU. I am sure John will take you there for a meal during your stay as well as in the Dining Hall at Chautauqua Park. As you can see, I am using notes I took from reading *Wikipedia*."

John interjects, "My father told me a story about the time he and his father, who ran a nursery, were contracted by the university to plant a variety of trees around the barren campus. Now these trees are fully grown or have been removed for new buildings. Also, one of the things I would like to do on Memorial Day is run in the 'BOLDER BOULDER,' a six-mile race through Boulder. It would be great if you could join me for the race. I know Bob has no interest participating in the event."

"You are correct, John. Even Betty does not have any desire to run in the strenuous race. Please tell us about Moscow and your university."

"As you know, the Russian capital is Moscow, the most populous city in Europe, about thirteen million. It was established in 1147 and is home to several UNESCO World Heritage Sites. John, I am sure you have visited Red Square, the Kremlin, and Saint Basil's Cathedral. You probably also saw the Moskva River that flows through the city and all the greenery in and around Moscow. It has the largest forest in an urban area, more than any other major city in the world.

"Mendeleev University of Chemical Technology is a public university that was founded in 1898. It is the largest higher educational institution and research center of chemistry and chemical engineering in the world. The university has several campuses that include two higher colleges, four institutions, and nine faculties. I teach chemical separations in the Faculty of Engineering Chemistry and Technology and even use the latest edition of your chemical separations book that was translated into Russian. You did a great job of writing the book, John."

"I need to return to work now. Please come to my office at five, Lara, and we can go to my home for dinner. If you wish following one of Betty's wonderful meals, you can try and get more sleep to help with your jet lag."

Back in their office, Lara tells John, "You sure resemble the Hollywood actor Tom Cruise, but taller. Indeed, your resemblance to Mr. Cruise is striking! You have his handsome features, enticing azure blue eyes and lustrous black hair, extraordinary physique, and an undeniable aura of machismo."

"Thank you, Lara. Indeed, both of my parents were good-looking, and the nice body they gave me does bring stares from women of all ages. You are indeed beautiful and charming and obviously highly intelligent being a tenured professor."

"I was also fortunate that my parents are intelligent, retired teachers in Moscow, and that my education in Moscow was first class. I also had a great advisor during my doctoral studies at Oxford. That is where I perfected my English and got to see a lot of the beautiful English countryside."

Later that afternoon, John takes Lara to his laboratory, where he introduces her to his three graduate students whom they will be supervising together. "Larry received his undergraduate degree from Florida State University, Susan's degree was awarded at Washington State University, and Mark graduated from the University of Melbourne, Australia. All three will be doing research in using new separation methods to treat radioactive wastewater and acidic mine water containing hazardous metals. We plan to obtain some water samples from major mines in Western Colorado and prepare simulated radioactive water. I also arranged to take them to the Actinide Separations Conference in San Diego at the end of March, where they will present poster papers on their research. Of course, you need to join us as I have plenty of travel funds in our Environmental Protection Agency contract."

"I would love to, especially since this is my first visit to the United States, and I want to see as much of your country that I can during my year here. I was lucky to visit several European cities during my studies at Oxford."

"Lara, maybe we could drive to California and visit some interesting cities and sites along the way. You three would have to fly since you need as much time in the laboratory as possible."

"That sounds wonderful, John."

The three students then take turns asking Lara about her university, students, and research. She ends her replies by saying that her student's research is in the same area as theirs. John and Lara then return to their office.

"CU's campus is certainly lovely, and the Flatirons are beautiful. The nice tour of Boulder and the campus that Bob gave me showed me how lucky I am to be able to have my sabbatical here. You certainly have a lot of interesting books on the shelves. Are the large ones all theses?"

"No, some are my annual diaries. I mainly write about the trips I took each year. You are welcome to borrow some to read if you want to."

"Thank you. I will take the latest one to read tonight or tomorrow night."

"There is a table of contents listing each trip, so it will be easy for you to select a trip you would like to read."

On Wednesday morning, Lara tells John that she really enjoyed reading about his trip to the Emirates and Iraq:

I left home for Denver International Airport via Uber about nine on Friday evening. The Uber driver was interesting as he related a few of his stories about other customers; his daytime job was an accounting manager for a firm in Downtown Denver.

My JetBlue flight left for New York at midnight. I had been assigned a middle seat in economy class and could not change it because it was a full flight; instead, I paid $50 for a third-row aisle seat in business class with the middle seat vacant. Following the four-hour flight to a cold and windy New York, I had about a five-hour wait for my Emirates flight to Dubai. The plane was an Airbus A380 double-decker; I lucked out as I got a three-seat row in economy class all to myself but still got little sleep. The flight to Dubai was almost thirteen hours, arriving Sunday morning at eight.

After arrival in Dubai and exchanging money (3.5 dirhams for $1), I took a short ride in a taxi to the four-star Al Seef Heritage Hotel, Curio Collection by Hilton. The unique hotel is in the Al Seef Heritage Area, old Fahidi District, near Dubai Creek (it is more like a broad river), and it sits among many old-style buildings. There are many interesting items in my room, which include bedside lamps inside old kerosene lanterns. The lobby has many antiques, including an Edison phonograph. The hotel consists of several buildings.

Following a four-hour nap, I had a walk in the Al Seef Contemporary and Heritage areas. Then I took a "hop-on hop-off" bus tour of the city that left from the Heritage Tower near the hotel. The tour bus went by many beautiful skyscrapers, the Dubai Museum and Mall, several hotels, the Old Souk, the Spice and Gold Souk, Deira City Center, and ended on the Sheikh Zayed Road. The halfway point was at the world's tallest building.

After the bus tour, I went for another walking tour of the small old city and saw many boats docked and traveling in the creek, and walked by numerous beautiful old buildings. My walk ended at the Skafos restaurant, where I had a wonderful dinner. Surprisingly, the restaurant served alcoholic drinks.

Following a good night's sleep, I took a taxi to the airport. The Dubai airport is big and modern with three terminals separated about ten blocks apart and connected by a subway. My terminal had about fifty gates with A to D wings and lots of shops. I had breakfast at Starbucks before flying to Iraq and starting the Spiekermann tour of ancient Mesopotamia and Jewels of Assyria.

Iraq became an independent country in 1932. Today it shares borders with Jordan, Kuwait, Saudi Arabia, Syria, the Gulf of Oman, and Turkey. The country's main topographical features are the Euphrates and Tigris rivers, which flow from Syria and Turkey in the north to the Gulf in the south. The northeast is mountainous, while the country in the west is arid desert. The land surrounding the two rivers is fertile plain, but the lack of effective irrigation has resulted in flooding and an area of marshland. Most of the country's economic, political, social, and physical infrastructures were destroyed during the 2003 war. However, a national election in December 2005 has brought increased stability to the country. The Iraqis are slowly rebuilding their country.

Owing to a long and varied history, Iraq is a culturally rich country. Mesopotamia, the land between the Euphrates and Tigris rivers, was home to the world's earliest civilization. Sites such as Eriu, Uruk, and Yr of the Chaldees and Babylon have traces of the first cultures to build cities, develop the wheel, invent writing, and rule the known world.

The Emirates flight to Basra was in a Boeing 777-300 with about five hundred seats that were mainly empty. Basra is important in terms of Iraq's and Islam's history and is surrounded by the largest plantation of date palms in the world. The canals that crisscross Basra have led to its being known as the Venice of the East. About forty miles north of Basra is Qurna at the junction of the Euphrates and Tigris rivers. According to legend, it is the site of the Garden of Eden.

At the Basra airport, following immigration, customs, and having my temperature measured by health personnel, I was met by our guide, Hida, and most of my traveling group. We were transported to the classy five-star Mnawi Basha Hotel located in the middle of the nice city of 1.7 million. The group consisted of Bill and Margie from the bay area; Bob from Oregon; Gary, a medical doctor from Florida; Helen from Australia; Jo and Jerry from West Arvada, Colorado (small world!); Joy from Austin, Texas, where she works for an insurance company; and Paul from Ireland.

The first morning, we boarded a small bus and went to the local hospital for a health check. On arrival, the first thing we saw was four men carrying a coffin from the hospital. The medical checking room was very crowded with sick people, but we were issued masks. Everyone in the group passed the health test that consisted of taking our temperatures and seeing that no one was coughing. After leaving the hospital and doing some shopping and money exchanging (1180 dinars for $1), we took a boat ride on the Shatt Al-Arab, which is the river following the merging of the Euphrates and the Tigris. In places on the shores were grounded many old and rusted ships of all sizes. On the drive around the nice city, I was surprised at the excellent condition of most buildings and the bridge over the wide river. I saw no war damage, and many buildings were being built. Surprisingly, we passed Gold's Gym and a building that looked like an American Pizza Hut, but it was called Pizza Home.

After breakfast on Tuesday, we went for some sightseeing in the old city along the stretch of the canal lined with old Ottoman Shenashil Houses. It is a sad shadow of Basra's former glory as most of them were unoccupied and falling apart. We then drove to Ali's steps, a mosque with an original minaret from the year 635. Unfortunately, we could not enter as it was closed. After a late lunch, we toured more of the city and did some shopping. The group received an excellent dinner at the hotel.

On Wednesday morning, we left the city to visit the ancient Mesopotamian town of Al-Qurnah. On the way out of the city, there were many roadside vendors selling a variety of goods and food. There were also lots of wrecked cars and trucks on the sides of the nice four-lane highway. Surprisingly, many of the cars on the highway were new or just a couple of years old. We also had to stop at two checkpoints on the way, where the police checked our passports. On the one-and-a-half-hour drive, we went from flat desert to marshland, where we saw lots of fishing taking place as well as many water buffalo, cattle, sheep, and chickens in trucks going to market. We also passed several small villages; most of the homes were made from cinder block.

Al-Qurnah is where the Euphrates and Tigris rivers meet and form the Shatt Al-Arab River. Nearby is the claimed site of the Garden of Eden that contains Adam's Tree, also known as the tree of knowledge. After a short visit, we drove to the nearby marshes for lunch in a private home. The Marsh Arabs live in these immense wetlands that are one of the largest ecosystems in the world. It also provides habitats for important wildlife populations. The Marsh Arabs, descendants of ancient Sumerians, live in secluded villages of elaborate reed houses that are reachable only by boat, and practice fishing, buffalo breeding, and reed weaving.

Following lunch, we went for a half-hour canoe ride. The group was placed in three canoes, where we saw a few water buffalo. I was a little worried as I could smell gasoline from a can feeding the engine, and the canoe pilot was smoking most of the trip. After the canoe ride, we boarded the bus and went to Nasiriya, the capital of the province of Dhi Qar, near the ruins of the ancient city of Ur on the Euphrates River. After arriving in Nasiriya, we had a stop to do some shopping in a new four-story shopping mall that is very impressive, much like our malls (such as the Flatirons Mall near Boulder). Besides many shops and several restaurants, it has a few entertainment features. There is a small electric train and artificial bears and lions that kids can ride on as well as a bowling alley.

After the mall visit and checking into the luxurious five-star Sumerian Hotel, we took a stroll around the souk of Nasiriya before dinner. The television evening news reported that two U.S. soldiers and one UK soldier were killed at a coalition base north of Baghdad by rocket fire from a rebel group supported by Iran. By the way, my spacious hotel room, containing beautiful furniture, is on the sixth floor with a great view of half of the spread-out city. Most of the other buildings are two-story.

The next day, we proceeded to drive to Babylon with gray skies and a little rain. In Babylon, we got to tour one of Saddam Hussein's several palaces that was abandoned. The large two-story building had been ransacked and graffitied. It sits near the Euphrates River and is surrounded by beautiful gardens. It would make a great hotel if it was restored. We were told that Saddam only visited the palace a couple of times.

After our arrival at a checkpoint on the outskirts of Baghdad, the police would not let us in, so our driver went to another checkpoint a mile or two away. There, our guide showed the police our passports and medical papers just like he had done at the first checkpoint. He argued with several of the police, and after about a half hour, they agreed to let us go to the airport but not to our hotel in the city. We were escorted by two police cars to the airport, and after arrival, they left us. Then our driver took us to the nice Baghdad hotel. I was surprised that the hotel had a bar serving alcoholic drinks. The bar was next to the restaurant, a pool table, and an indoor swimming pool.

The next morning, our host and driver took me and five others of our group to the Baghdad airport. The security at the airport was the most thorough I had ever experienced. A mile from the airport, the bus was searched and examined for explosives by a dog. A few blocks later, we had to board a small van and driven to another checkpoint, where another dog sniffed our suitcases. Next, we had to go through the first of three more metal detectors with our shoes off and have our baggage X-rayed. Before boarding the plane, a final security check was performed. The flight left Baghdad at eleven and arrived in Dubai at two in the afternoon. (Dubai is an hour ahead of Baghdad.) After our arrival and updating my ticket, I went to the plush two-story airport hotel that is in the middle terminal building. After I checked my e-mail and helped myself to free food and drink in their café, I went to my room and got a few hours' sleep. The next morning, I also got a free breakfast before going to my departure gate.

A little after eight on Monday morning, I boarded a Boeing 777 for an Emirates Air flight to Boston. I paid to upgrade to business class since I had been assigned a middle seat in economy class, and there were no aisle or window seats available on the full flight. In business class, I had a window seat and got all the food and drink I wanted. During the thirteen-hour flight, I did not get any sleep despite being able to recline my seat to a horizontal position. I did watch three movies and played some chess on the plane's computer.

We arrived in Boston at two in the afternoon. The immigration officer asked me a lot of questions, mainly about what I did in Iraq. The airport was not crowded, unlike the Dubai airport. I had a four-hour wait for my flight to Denver. I paid JetBlue $50 for a seat in business class, where the only perk was more legroom. It appeared that JetBlue has a hub in Boston since their planes occupied a whole concourse out of six of them. Following the five-hour flight, I took an Uber home.

"John, I have one question about your trip. Did you need a visa for Iraq?"

"Yes, but Spiekermann Travel Service obtained it for me."

"I am sure it was an adventure for you. I think I would be afraid to go on the trip because of terrorism."

"Well, there were a few times I questioned our group's safety, especially our stops in deserted parts of the desert. By the way, you are welcome to borrow more of my diaries if you wish to read about a few more of my trips. I would also recommend reading this book, *The Bare Essentials*, a book that my first wife wrote. The story involves a CU chemistry professor who goes to the University of Vienna for a year's sabbatical. His friend, who is head of the analytical laboratory of Warsaw's Nuclear Energy Institute, asks him to analyze samples of natural gas to see if the gas contains mind-altering drugs. He suspects that the drugs are being introduced by your country to subdue the Polish people during the Cold War. The professor agrees to perform the analysis but is unaware that by doing so, he will subject both himself and his Polish-born wife to acts of terror, including an attempt on his life."

III

After their start on the seventeen-mile drive to Nederland through Boulder Canyon that parallels Boulder Creek, John asks Lara to tell him a little more about herself. "Well, I grew up in Moscow with an older brother and wonderful parents and attended public schools until my university studies. My father was a chemistry professor at Mendeleev, and my mother taught chemistry at a nearby high school. Both are now retired. I think I told you that I did my undergraduate studies at Mendeleev and then went to Oxford University for my PhD, doing research in chemical separations. We used the first edition your book, *Chemical Separations*, in one of my classes. After returning to Moscow, my father arranged a postdoc position for me at Mendeleev and later a position as a lecturer. Over the years, I worked my way up to full professor. During this time, I had a short marriage to Ivan Medvedev, who was a police officer. He was a very jealous and violent man, and after two years of his abuse, I divorced him. For many months after the divorce, he continued to harass me and even threatened to kill me. He said on many occasions that I would always be his wife. Finally, he left me alone after I got a restraining order. It was indeed a very dark time in my life. I used to refer to him as Ivan the Terrible to my friends. Since then I have avoided getting serious about a second marriage. I also moved back to my parents' apartment to help them.

"My travels are just a small fraction of the number of your trips. Of course, I have seen some of Western Russia, and when I was in England, I toured the countryside near Oxford and London. The highlight was seeing Stonehenge. I also enjoyed visiting Paris, Brussels, Amsterdam, Luxembourg, Frankfurt, and Northern Ireland. I will tell you about the Ireland trip on our return to Boulder."

"The summary of my life so far is a little longer than your story. I grew up with wonderful parents and two brothers and two sisters in a two-bedroom home in West Denver. I attended elementary and junior high schools near our home and West High at the edge of Downtown Denver. In high school, my grades dropped since I became more interested in cars and girls than education. I also worked at a supermarket part time. I dropped out of high school during my senior year to work more but went back the following year and graduated. I then started college studies at CU Denver part time and started working full time at Rocky Flats as a janitor.

"The Rocky Flats Plant was between here and Golden off Highway 93. Parts for nuclear weapons were made there for many years, but now the plant is no longer there. It was decontaminated and demolished several years ago. Now the area is a national wildlife refuge.

"During the next three years at Rocky Flats, I was promoted to laboratory technician, and I continued part-time studies at CU Denver, majoring in chemistry. I then took a two-year leave of absence from Rocky Flats and attended classes full time during my junior and senior years on the Boulder campus. Following being awarded a bachelor of science degree in chemistry, I returned to Rocky Flats as a full-time chemist in the research and development department and continued going to CU Boulder full time for my masters, doctoral, and postdoctoral studies. After my university studies, I was promoted to manager of a group in the department and later director of the department.

"I met Margrit Hoffman when I was in graduate school. We only had a three-month courtship before we were married. She was a beautiful, wonderful lady, and we were lucky to eventually have three great children, Amy, Eric, and Lorrie. I am sure you will get to meet my adult children sometime soon. Margrit was killed in an automobile accident when we lived in California."

"John, I am so sorry to hear that. Please continue."

"Over two decades ago, I spent three years at the International Atomic Energy Agency in Vienna, Austria. In my previous work at Rocky Flats, I was a contributor to the development of the neutron bomb. In Vienna, KGB agents were trying to get information for the bomb from me via Margrit. She became romantically involved with Andrei Pushkin, thought by the CIA to be a KGB agent. Realizing the futility of their relationship, Margrit told me about Andrei and how they unsuccessfully attempted to terminate it. Later, Andrei committed suicide, and Margrit was beside herself with grief, but that event saved our marriage. Later, I was to find out that Andrei had faked his suicide and left Vienna for Canada to start a new life. After leaving the agency, Margrit, our three children, and I returned to our home in Arvada. Margrit and I resumed a close, loving relationship that had been severely damaged in Vienna. I also returned to Rocky Flats as manager of the Plutonium Chemistry Research and Development Group.

"About this time, I traveled a lot to conferences overseas and to Vienna and Moscow to have meetings with my two Russian coauthors on a series of books we were writing for the IAEA. Following more contacts with my Russian colleagues, I was informed that a background investigation had been conducted by the Department of Energy and the FBI. This investigation resulted in me losing my security clearance. I then went to Australia to teach for three years and later to work in California for three years. Andrei came to California and tried to renew his relationship with Margrit and kill me, but instead, he accidentally killed Margrit. I found out later that he committed suicide in Canada and told his son, Alex, in his dying breath that I had shot him.

"At that point, I wanted to start a new life and left California for a teaching job at Clemson University in South Carolina. I even started using my middle name, James. I enjoyed the academic life very much, supervising several students and teaching actinide chemistry. I even purchased the car and home that Margrit liked.

"Alex joined my research group using a different last name. I did not know that he was Andrei's youngest son. In early January, two years ago, I took him, two other graduate students, and Ying, a postdoctoral student from China, with me on an expedition to Antarctica, where we would do some ice sampling. By that time, I had fallen in love with Ying. We were married by the ship's captain as we crossed the Antarctic Circle. The following night, me, Alex, and a dozen other brave souls camped out on Hovgaard Island, where there was an attempt on my life. On the last night of the trip, as we were crossing the Drake Passage and heading past Cape Horn, the sea was very rough, and large waves were coming over the front of the ship. Alex met me at the stern of the ship and with difficulty admitted that his real name was Alexander Pushkin, that his father was the one who had a love affair with Margrit in Vienna, and that his father had cut the break lines on my car in California with the intention of killing me and not Margrit. I was shocked as Alex admitted that on the camping night, he was the one who had kicked the rock that was holding me and my sleeping bag in place. As I was sliding down the hill, Alex told me that he was immediately sorry for what he had done and ran trying to stop me, but I had managed to stop myself at the edge of the hill above the sea. He also said that his father shot himself in his home in Canada where he was staying, and his father told him in his dying breath that I had shot him and that he should kill me. I sternly told Alex that I did not kill his father and have an alibi. Alex agreed and told me he learned that morning that his father had committed suicide. Alex told me that he was extremely sorry that he had tried to kill me. At the end of our conversation, I told Alex that under the circumstances, I forgive him. My last words were for him to come and give me a big bear hug. Alex happily jumped over and gave me a hardy embrace that caused both of us to accidentally fall over the back of the ship into the rough, freezing ocean."

John then tells Lara about Deborah saving his life, about his year in Chile, falling in love with Deborah, getting his memory back, and returning to South Carolina. "Upon my return to the U.S., Ying and I resumed our lives together, and I went back to teaching at Clemson. But later, Alex's brother arrived in Clemson, trying to kill me but instead killed Ying in a similar manner as Margrit's death. A week later, he also attempted a second time to kill me but failed.

"In trying to get over my loss of Ying, I slowly renewed a loving relationship with Deborah, and we started traveling in South America. Several months later, while back in Clemson, I was invited to speak at an international conference in Moscow. I invited Deborah to join me, and we first went to Vienna, where we were married. After our arrival in Moscow and my attending the conference all week, Deborah and I enjoyed the banquet on the last night of the conference. After returning to our room that night, Alex's brother surprised me and Deborah with a gun and shot both of us. Immediately after being shot, I jump over to the brother, giving him a bear hug, trying to wrestle the gun from him. During the scuffle, the gun fired a third time, killing him.

"The police and ambulance came and took Deborah and I to the nearby hospital, where we were operated on to remove the bullets and then placed in intensive care. I survived, but Deborah did not.

"After Deborah's passing, I had another attempt on my life in the hospital that nearly succeeded, but I had a good nurse that did an excellent job of CPR on me. I knew it was Andrei's brother that tried to kill me, and I told that to the police.

"After returning to Clemson, I had several e-mail exchanges with Misa, my best Russian friend. He wrote that the police continued their search for the brother but with no success thus far, and he would continue to keep me informed. I also arranged for a realtor to sell my two homes in South Carolina, and when I was ready, I called for movers to come and load my furniture and personal things for transport to Nederland. I then drove to Colorado so I could start a new life here."

"John, I am so sorry about the death of your wife and the attempts on your life. Do you have any concerns about another attempt?"

"Hopefully not since I do not think Andrei's brother knows where I work and live now. By the way, I know your country well. The IAEA sponsored trips for me to go to Moscow several times to work on a series of books two Russian professors and I were writing for the agency. Margrit was with me on the first trip to Moscow, where we first visited Stockholm, Helsinki, and Leningrad. I also took the train from Vladivostok to Moscow, and on the trip, I spent a day at Lake Baikal. It was a great train ride."

As they pass an intersection on the right, John says, "That is the road to the old mining town of Gold Hill that consists of a restaurant and bar, store, and a few homes. There are two roads going out of Gold Hill, one to the Peak to Peak Highway and the other one back to Boulder."

A little farther up Boulder Canyon, they pass a road on the left. Lara asks, "Where does that road go?"

"That road eventually ends in Nederland. Near the west end of the road, that is called Magnolia Drive, is where the Jefferson County Open Space trail from Pine Shadows ends.

"I have told you about the several trips I have made to Moscow and my train trip from Vladivostok to Moscow, but let me tell you about the trip I made to Kamyshin, Russia, a small city on the Volga River between Volgograd and Saratov, where my mother's father emigrated from in 1910. I do not know much about my mother's mom except that she was also of Russian ancestry.

"I flew into Sheremetyevo Airport from Berlin then transferred to a flight to Volgograd. I stayed in Volgograd at the Ruefa Hotel for three nights. The first morning, I arranged for a taxi to take me to Kamyshin, a four-hour drive. The landscape was beautiful on the drive. The highway paralleled the Volga river about half of the time. Kamyshin is a nice compact city with a long bridge going over the Volga river. We went to the town's historical museum, but I did not find any information about my mom's father or grandfather. After two hours in Kamyshin, we headed back to Volgograd.

"I spent most of the next day taking a long walk around Volgograd. There is a beautiful church near the hotel that has unique architecture. As I was there, the bells of the church started to ring, so I went inside the church, named Kazansky Sobor, and a service was just starting. It was a different type of service. People were just standing around as the choir was singing and organ playing. There were two priests walking around spreading incense, and the people would bow at different times. Some would kiss pictures on the pillars. All the women and children were wearing scarfs. The inside of the church is beautiful, and the service was divine. The next morning, I flew back to Moscow and stayed there two nights before flying to Berlin then home."

"Wow, John, I think you have seen more of Russia than I have."

John then tells Lara a little about Nederland. "During the 1850s, the town started as a trading post between European settlers and Ute Indians, and in 1874, it was officially established. The town's first economic boom started with gold, silver, and tungsten discoveries in Eldora, Caribou, and east of the town. I plan to take you to see Caribou and the Eldora Ski Area. The town's name came from the Nederland Mining Company, headquartered in the Netherlands, which bought the Caribou Mine."

"What is the elevation and population of Nederland, John?"

"The town's elevation is 8,234 feet above sea level, and the population is almost two thousand. The Continental Divide is 8 miles west of Nederland, and Barker Reservoir is on the west side of town. Boulder Creek runs through the reservoir, supplying Boulder with its drinking water. The Peak to Peak Highway goes through the town from Blackhawk to Estes Park, some of the towns I would like to take you to if you are interested."

"Yes, of course."

"The main recreational attractions for visitors to Nederland are the nearby Indian Peaks and James Peak Wilderness areas and the Roosevelt National Forest. The town's cultural events are an annual music and arts festival, Miners Day celebration, and Frozen Dead Guy Days. The latter one commemorates a Norwegian immigrant freezing his father cryogenically to bring him back to life once medical science reached that point. The desire to leave his father in a frozen coffin gave the town a lot of publicity, including CNN televising a baker holding a sign with the words 'What is the big deal about a Norwegian in the freezer? I have six Danish in the oven.'"

John smiles as Lara laughs.

"Of course, later, the town capitalized on the situation by having Frozen Dead Guy Days with coffin races, dead guy look-alike costumes, and other crazy and deadly activities. By the way, the frozen guy is just two doors west of Pine Shadows on Doe Trail."

"Why do you call your home Pine Shadows?"

"It is because the house sits on the shady side of the mountain and is mostly covered by the shadows of the many pine trees behind the house."

As they are starting to drive past Barker Reservoir, John says, "Can you see my house and garage now? It is the highest one on the north side of the mountain."

"Yes, your big white house is easy to see, and it sure stands out among the smaller homes west of your home."

They drive through Nederland and make a left-hand turn onto Big Springs Drive and then another left turn onto Alpine Drive to Doe Trail that ends on the southeast corner of Nederland. The almost three-mile ride is on a gravel road. "I think it is interesting that my house has the address '86 Doe Trail' since I lost my DOE security clearance in 1986."

"When did you start building the house?"

"It was several years after I purchased the land, when I had more money."

After arriving at Pine Shadows, John and Lara walk to the garage and climb the steel and concrete stairs to the front deck. After admiring the wonderful westerly view of the Continental Divide, Eldora Ski Area, Barker Reservoir, and Nederland, they go through a patio doorway into John's living room. Deborah says, "This is a beautiful large room with a nice dining area and spacious kitchen. I love your furniture and the fireplace."

John then shows her both bedrooms with bathrooms as well as the laundry room and stairs that are behind the kitchen. "John, I find all your maps, pictures, and awards on your walls very interesting."

"As you can see, both bedrooms have patio doors that go onto the large front-covered deck that also serves as the roof of the carport for three autos. Whit, Red, and Gail's car rest in the garage, and Randy parks his Jeep Wrangler in the carport behind Gail's car since he is usually the first to leave in the morning and the last one to come home. There is a large workshop and storage area in front of where the three cars sit as well as a door leading to the covered patio, where I have my exercise machine and weights, a jacuzzi, some outdoor furniture, and a ping-pong/pool table. The patio has windows around the top half of the walls and a patio door in the middle of the east side. A little farther east is my tennis court and swimming pool. Do you play tennis or shoot pool?"

"You will have to teach me tennis, and I am not good at playing ping-pong or shooting pool. I do love to play chess though. Do you?"

"That is one of my favorite games as well as a card game called Crazy Eight. I also like to play Scrabble. Let me show you the first floor of the house now, where you will hopefully be living."

After taking the short walk to the house that faces to the northwest, John explains, "The house is much like the rental home I designed and helped build in South Carolina, except it is larger. The upper two floors are identical to this floor and my apartment over the garage. You could use the second bedroom as your office. As you saw, my office has a desk, bookcases, and a sleeper couch for overnight guests."

"Both the house and garage have fire-resistant siding and solar collectors on the metal roofs. There are also sprinkler systems in all the rooms as required by the county building code. The code also requires a large open area around structures. As you saw, I have rock gardens in those areas. I especially like the Southern Colonial appearance of the house with the four large white pillars holding up the extended roof that covers the top-floor deck. The extended roof also keeps the second-floor deck and front patio dry. From all three levels, one has the same lovely views as from the apartment deck. There are dormers above each of the three patio doors on the top floor. The ten-acre property is next to Jefferson County Open Space, with a walking trail that I mentioned to you. By the way, my renters have invited us for lunch."

After John shows Lara the other rooms, they go out the front patio door onto the concrete patio and admire the view. After several minutes there, they walk up the outside steel and concrete stairs to the second-floor deck. After a knock on the middle patio door, Randy comes and lets them into the living room. John then introduces Lara to Gail and Randy. Then they all sit, and John starts the conversation by asking Randy and Gail to briefly tell Lara about their lives.

Randy starts by saying, "We moved here from Boulder shorty after John built this house. We love the home and the area, especially since it is close to my job. I am a climate scientist working at the University of Colorado Institute of Arctic and Alpine Research Field Station, at 9,500 feet and about 7 miles north of Nederland on Highway 72, also called the Peak to Peak Highway. After reaching the turn off to the institute, one must drive west a little over a mile on a gravel washboard road to get there. The institute has two main buildings. The largest building contains offices and classrooms, and the other one houses research laboratories. I have worked there since graduating from CU over two decades ago. You are welcome to come for a visit anytime."

Gail then briefly tells the group about herself. "I am a realtor in Nederland and can work from home a lot. We have two teenage boys that attend Nederland Middle and High School. I also love the area and this home. The whole family snowboards at Eldora a lot, and we hike the trails on many summer days. The adjoining trail as well as the other one closer to town are our favorites. Every once in a while, I see the same pair of deer in the nearby woods. Once there was a bear trying to dig up some of our garbage that Randy buried in the vegetable garden. We do put our trash in a bear-proof bin. We also got rid of our bird feeders since we were told they also attract bears. John's good friends, the Cochins, told us they get deer, elk, and sometime a moose in their backyard. They have a big lovely home on twenty acres a few miles north of Nederland that we got to visit a few times."

Following Lara telling the group about herself and having lunch, Gail gives Lara a tour of the second and third levels while John and Randy chat in the living room. Their two boys who share the top floor are in school. John and Lara conclude the visit to the house by thanking Randy and Gail for the lunch. They then take a short walk around part of the property where the snow has melted.

"How would you like to see Nederland now and some of the surrounding area?"

"That sounds great, John. I certainly love the apartment, and your home and property are wonderful, especially the large decks on the front of both buildings with the great views. I look forward to living here for a year. I hope I can move in as soon as possible."

"Why don't we go and pick out your furniture at a store in Boulder later so we can hopefully have it delivered tomorrow while I am at home? You will need to buy a bed, sofa, desk, and table and chairs. As you saw, all the kitchen appliances are already installed as well as the washer and dryer. Friday night you can move in with your luggage."

"I will call Bob and let him know I will not be back for dinner. Perhaps we can eat somewhere before I buy the furniture."

"If it's okay, I can help you select the furniture since I am sure you will leave it behind after you return to Moscow."

"Of course, John. I will be buying the furniture for you so I can have a lovely furnished apartment for a year. Of course, as you offered, the cost of the furniture will be in exchange for no rent money."

"Before we head back to Boulder a different way, via the mining towns of Blackhawk, Central City, and Idaho Springs, let me show you briefly around Nederland now."

After a walk down the three blocks of Nederland's old town and short visits to Eldora Ski Area and the old mining town of Eldora, they travel to Blackhawk. During the twenty-minute drive, John tells Lara about some of his boyhood days with trips to the area with his friends and friends of Bill, his elder brother, who had cars. "We did a lot fishing at lakes and streams and took many hikes on the trails in the mountain valleys, looking for minerals. I could name most of the minerals we found. At the time, I had quite a mineral collection that I displayed in my one-room chemistry laboratory that Bill and I built. It was in our backyard, and I used to do lots of experimenting there. My interest in chemistry first started after receiving a chemistry set on my tenth birthday. A couple of years later, we used the lumber from the one-room lab and some I had to buy to build a larger two-room laboratory. At the time, I was buying more and more chemicals and laboratory equipment with the money I earned from cutting lawns."

"It sounds like your love for chemistry started at an early age. My interest in chemistry was sparked by doing chemical experiments in my high school chemistry class. Of course, my parents were a great influence on my career in chemistry."

"After I started driving my own car and joining a hot rod club, my interest in chemistry faded but came back after I started working at Rocky Flats as a laboratory technician. Then I was determined to become a chemistry professor someday and started attending evening classes at CU's Denver Center."

After reaching Blackhawk and parking Red, they have a stroll around the gambling town and take short visits to two casinos. Following a short drive to the adjoining historic town of Central City, they go into one of the casinos that John suggests since he had some good luck at the slot machines in the past. However, Lara loses some money on the machines. Next, they drive to Idaho Springs so John can show Lara another mining town. On the way, he tells Lara about the time he and Margrit hosted three Russian friends who were in Denver to attend an international solvent extraction conference. "We took our three friends to the top of the highest mountain road in the U.S., Mount Evans, followed by showing them Central City. As I was taking my friends on the town tour, Margrit had a newspaper printed in a souvenir shop with the headlines 'Soviet Spies Arrested in Central City.' Our friends got a lot of laughs over the newspaper, and Margrit gave the paper to Misa to take back to Moscow."

"Well, John, I am glad you did not have a newspaper printed for me. If you would have, what would have been the headlines?"

"Maybe 'Beautiful Russian Professor Loses Lots of Money at the Slot Machines.' Or maybe 'Slot Machine Beats Beautiful Russian Visitor.'"

"John, you sure are lots of fun to be with. I am so happy that we are officemates and that we will also be neighbors."

"Thank you, and I am also pleased that I get to spend some time with a very remarkable lady. Maybe you can help me improve the little Russian that I know. By the way, how would you like to join me for a meal at my son's home on Saturday followed by a visit to the Wild Animal Sanctuary north of the airport?"

"Well, I will have to cancel many engagements with my numerous friends. Ha ha. You are the only real friend I have since the other faculty members I have met all spend their leisure time with their families."

"As you know, I have been invited for breakfast at the Stevens' on Friday morning, where, of course, you will be eating. Following breakfast will be a good time to put your luggage in my car for transport to Pine Shadows after work. We will have another faculty meeting on Monday, where you will have to discuss the research you have under way. I think Bob will want you to give the seminar talk a week from Friday."

"Thank you for the warning. It will be easy for me to talk about the research, and at the seminar, I will discuss the work I have done at Mendeleev as well as my planned investigations in your laboratory. Of course, most of my research will be related to the student's work that you have asked me to assist you with."

On their drive back to Boulder following their short visit to Idaho Springs, Lara tells John about her trip to Northern Ireland. "I arrived in Belfast on an early morning flight from London. One of the city's principal landmarks was seen upon arrival, the two Harland & Wolff cranes, nicknamed Samson and Goliath. It was there that many great ships were built, including the *Olympic*, *Britannic*, and the RMS *Titanic*. After a tour of Belfast, our tour group proceeded to the town of Carrickfergus by bus for a short photo stop, and then the bus took the coast road north through the picturesque fishing village of Carnlough. We continued passing the coastal villages of Glenariff, Cushendall, and Cushendun. There were stunning views of the sea to the right and the mountains to the left. Most impressive were the spectacular views of Mull of Kimntyre, Scotland. Moving inland, we came to the town of Ballycastle, home to Ireland's oldest town fair. Our next stop was at the famous Carrick-a-Rede Rope Bridge. Its construction facilitated the local fishermen access to Sheep Island, where there is excellent fishing. The walk to the swinging bridge was up a hill then down on stone steps. Going over the bridge was quite scary. We then headed for Dunluce Castle for a photo stop before arriving at the Giant's Causeway. There are about forty thousand interlocking basalt columns there as a result of a volcanic eruption. After leaving the Giant's Causeway, we returned to Belfast, taking a different route."

"That sounds like you had a great trip, Lara. Years ago, I had a short visit to Belfast that was very enjoyable. I especially liked the *Titanic* museum."

After their return to Boulder, they have dinner at the Dark Horse, Lara's first visit to the unique restaurant and bar with lots of collectibles hanging on the walls and from the ceiling. John tells Lara about the place and how he used to have safety meetings there when he worked at Rocky Flats. After the meal, they went to a nearby furniture store and picked out the furniture for Lara. "John, I am so happy you liked the pieces I chose. I am also pleased that the furniture can be delivered in the morning while you are at home."

"I am happy that you are happy. Now its past my bedtime, and I will drop you at the Stevens'."

On Friday, John arrives at the Stevens' home for breakfast. Over the meal, John tells Lara and the Stevens, "Lara's furniture safely arrived yesterday at Pine Shadows and was arranged in the first floor of my house, where she will be living this year."

"Thank you so much, John. I think Nederland is great, and your home is superb. I sure like the furniture we bought."

"By the way, Lara and I have been invited to have a meal at my son's home tomorrow and visit the Wildlife Animal Sanctuary near the Denver airport. Have you been there?"

"Bob and I have not, but it is on our 'to do' list."

"Your meals are so delicious, Betty. I will certainly miss your wonderful cooking. You and Bob have been so kind to put me up since I arrived in Colorado."

"Lara, it has been our pleasure, and perhaps someday we will visit you in Moscow, where you can return the favor. Please put your suitcases in John's car now since I need to get to the office."

John and Lara give their thanks to Betty for a wonderful breakfast and depart for campus. Over lunch in the Packer Grill, Lara tells John, "Before going to bed last night, I read about another one of your wonderful trips. This one was your trip to Nepal."

On Monday, November 18, at 7:30 a.m., I was picked up by an Uber driver and driven to DIA via HY-76 to Ninety-Sixth Avenue to Pena Blvd. Since there was lot of construction on I-70, that would have made the drive much longer if we had gone that way. Anyway, it took about an hour. I boarded my Canadian Air flight at 10:40 a.m. I had a nice traveling companion on the flight. Virginia is a Canadian who lives in Newfoundland. She had spent a week with her daughter who lives in Arvada. Virginia was nice to talk with, and she and I exchanged stories of our travels. Across the aisle was a young lady with a child less than six months. The baby was very entertaining. He laughed at all my funny faces. We arrived in Toronto at 3:44 p.m. Then I went through the airport to the international terminal as an in-transit passenger. There was a two-hour loss of time. I had a long layover, and my flight to Istanbul did not leave until 10:30 p.m.—a wait of almost seven hours. During the wait, I had dinner, wrote in this diary, and finished editing what I had written so far on the general chemistry textbook. The Turkish Air flight to Istanbul was almost ten hours, arriving at four in the afternoon on November 19. In Istanbul, the layover was about nine hours, so I got a small room in the airport hotel. The room had a king-size bed and bathroom. As usual, however, I could not sleep. At 1:30 a.m., November 20, I flew to Kathmandu on Turkish Air, arriving at 11:00 a.m. On the landing approach, I and the other passengers, on the right side of the plane, could see a beautiful snowcapped mountain range. After landing at Kathmandu airport, which is small, we had to deplane on stairs and went by bus to the terminal.

Kathmandu, the capital of Nepal, is spread out with many two- to ten-story buildings and an area of shanties. It has a population of about four million and an elevation of 3,900 feet above sea level. Nepal is slightly larger than New York state and has a population of about thirty million, of which 82 percent are Hindu. The country is rich in culture and religion. It is a landlocked country located between China and India, with eight of the world's highest peaks, including Mount Everest and Kanchenjunga.

Following immigration (where I paid $30 for a fifteen-day visa), I and many others (about half Chinese tourists) went through a baggage area and customs to the outside. There, I was met by my driver and guide (Bijayl) in an Indian vehicle, something like a jeep that seats six. Sandhyp was also with Bijayl. I started calling them Sandy and BJ. Emily and Bob Smith had arrived earlier on a Dubai Airline flight from Boston via Dubai. Bob is a retired attorney who *worked for the trade industry in Boston. Emily is a retired schoolteacher (history).*

After arrival at the Kaze Darbar hotel, a heritage building with restaurant and a courtyard (where yoga is performed each morning at seven), BJ checked me in. I then went to my room. The accommodations are nice, but all entryways are a little lower than my six-foot height, so I must take care not to hit my head.

Following a late lunch of chicken soup, I met BJ, Sandy, Bob, and Emily in the restaurant, where we discussed the plans of the Global Exchange trip: "Nepal: the Dalit Movement's Struggle" and reviewed the cultural orientation information and the health and safety guidelines. I gave BJ a small souvenir football with "Broncos – Denver" on it for his five-year-old son. Later that afternoon, BJ took us to a money exchange booth in the middle of the city, where I exchanged $200 for 22,680 rupees. I felt rich, about 110 rupees per U.S. dollar. After dinner, we went to see the World Heritage Site, "the Great Boudha Stupa," known as Khastrit, which is about one hundred feet high. After my group and I had a walk around the Stupa as well as the area where there were many Buddhist statues, we returned to the hotel for the night.

On day 2, I woke at six and organized my luggage, wrote about the trip so far, and went to breakfast at eight. Later, Bob and Emily joined me. Then BJ came along, and we discussed the plans for the day. Our first visit would be to Patan Durbar Square, a UNESCO World Heritage Site, where there were many beautiful temples, including the Golden Temple (Hiranya Varna Mahavihar) in Lalitpur. The historical Buddhist monastery has a large museum containing many big and small statues of Buddha. From 1934 to 1958, the palace was used as a jail. Some buildings were still damaged from the earthquakes of 1934 and 2015. By the way, Buddhism started in Nepal then spread to Asia.

Following the morning visits and a nice lunch, we went to the Samata Foundation to learn how they advocate against caste-based discrimination and untouchability. The group met with the founder of the Darnal Award for social justice, the executive chairperson for the Samata Foundation, and an assistant, also with the Samata Foundation. Their main work deals with the Dalit community. One thing we learned was that some of the people with certain surnames are discriminated against.

Our final stop was meeting a lecturer at the university over dinner to learn of the history of Nepal with a special focus on the religion and caste system in Nepal as well as the origin of the caste system. I was surprised to hear that the ruling political party is the Communist party.

After breakfast on day 3, Friday, November 22, we had a second visit to the Samata Foundation to have another meeting with the managing director and executive chairperson. We discussed the status of Dalit women in Nepal and learned more about the issues of Dalit women.

Next, we went to the nice and big American Embassy to hear from the political officer about the plight of Dalit women from the perspective of the U.S. in Nepal. The officer's assistant gave an excellent presentation.

Following the visit to the embassy, we went to the National Human Rights Commission to hear about their activities from the deputy director of the organization; she was educated as an attorney.

Our last stop of the day was a meeting with the president of the Feminist Dalit Organization and vice chairperson of the Asia Dalit Rights Forum. She had a lot of awards in her office, including a picture of her and President Carter during his visit here ten years ago.

We ended the day with a walk around Swayambhunath World Heritage Site. There are numerous Buddha statues there overlooking the city; it was a good place to see how large the city is. It was fun to watch the antics of the monkeys playing around the site. I had never seen so many young and old monkeys running around and fighting over the food the visitors were throwing at them. There were also at least a dozen dogs running around but not fighting with the monkeys.

The next morning, after an early breakfast, Bob arrived and told me and BJ that Emily was sick with Montezuma's revenge and had vomited all night and had diarrhea. Thus, we postponed our long drive to the Aapshawara Village and stayed in town. We did have some remarkable visits though. The first one was to Swayambhu Mahachaitya. The Swayambhu Stupa is most impressive, and we saw lots of monkeys running around with a few dogs. We also went to see the Temple of Pashupatinath, next to the Bagmati River, and saw several other temples and lots of monkeys. There were two dead bodies rapped in cloth in the river for some type of ritual before cremation. In the afternoon, we went to Devapattan, Kathmandu, to see the many temples there. We ended the day with a pizza dinner at the Roadhouse Café.

Before we left the city on Sunday, November 24 (day 5), for Aapshawara Village, we took Bob and Emily to the Traveler's Hospital so Emily could get some treatment for her sick condition. Bob would stay in town the rest of the trip looking after Emily. In leaving Kathmandu, the smog was bad, traffic terrible, and Coca-Cola signs were everywhere. On the drive to the village were many beautiful tree-covered hills and mountains.

The homestay village was in Tanahun District, ninety miles from the capital. Upon arrival at the homestay family home, BJ and I had to walk up a steep hill on flat stone steps to the home. The driver was going to stay in the nearby town. The homestay house is part of a small farm and has two stories with a separate cooking room (wood fire) and outhouse (only a pit, no toilet). BJ and I could only enter our bedroom from the outside, and the doorway was just like the hotel—we had to duck to get in and out of the room. Of course, we also had to remove our shoes at the porch before going into the bedroom. The front yard was dirty and muddy in some places. We had our meals at a small table in the front yard. There were two twin gray cats, two dogs, a dozen chickens, goat, pigs, cow, and a buffalo running around the farm.

We were greeted by the Dalit family: grandmother, mother, father, and three daughters. There were also two darling two-year-old boys, always running around and entertaining everyone. They enjoyed the rubber balls I had brought from the U.S. as gifts. In the evening, several neighbors came so I could have an opportunity to learn about their work and various issues related to caste systems.

I had a rough night sleeping in a double bed with a three-inch hard mattress and a hard pillow. BJ was sharing the room with me and slept fine on a single bed. After a nice breakfast outside, BJ and I gave our thanks and goodbyes to the family.

After picking up Sandy, we had a long drive to Hemja (lunch on the way), a town near Pokhara. After getting off the main paved road, we went up a five-mile rocky, muddy, and rough road to Astham, where we would stay one night at the Annapurna Eco Village. The small village sits on a mountain 21,000 feet high with beautiful views of the Annapurna Himalayan mountain range. At the village, there are several groups of bungalows with flat stone roofs, each one with a bedroom and bathroom. To take a shower, one must go to the kitchen (located with the reception and dining room) and get a bucket of warm water and go to a small enclosed area outside to wash. That afternoon, I had a walkabout in the nearby village that has about a dozen homes on small farms. It looked like everyone had gardens. I also spent some time taking in the breathtaking view of the Annapurna Himalayan range. The dozen guests at the eco village were from Australia and Canada. After dinner, I signed the guest book and saw that most of the former guests were German, Swiss, and even a few from Oregon. During the night, I got very cold and had to add another blanket and wear my hat and put my socks, pants, shirt, and light jacket over my pajamas. BJ and Sandy also had their own separate bungalows.

Following breakfast on day 7, Tuesday, November 26, we drove to Pokhara, Nepal's most popular tourist city. Before arriving in Pokhara, we stopped to see a monastery and school for young monks. There are about a dozen buildings at the monastery, including a temple and many classrooms.

After arriving in Pokhara, we checked into the first-class Portland Hotel. The city is nice with lots of hotels, restaurants, shops, and spas as well as a Baskin-Robbins and KFC. The World Peace Pagoda is also located in the city. Following lunch at Rosemary's, I had a ninety-minute massage with scrub for $30. Later, the three of us had a walk about the town full of tourists.

Following breakfast at the hotel the next day, we went for a long walk around the city and spent some time at the large Fewa Lake with an island. Barah Temple is located on the island. We took an interesting boat ride to the island. There were lots of boats on the lake and many fishermen around the shores. We had lunch at Godfathers Pizza, followed by several games of pool. After more walking around town and an early dinner at Fresh Elements, where they had excellent food, we retired for the night.

After breakfast, we started our six-hour drive back to Kathmandu. We traveled on a paved two-lane curvy road paralleling a river through several small villages. In the villages were lots of school kids waiting for buses and a few dogs and cows on the road. About halfway to Kathmandu, we stopped at a first-class resort with three floors of rooms, restaurant, tennis court, swimming pool, and sleeping tents in the lawn area. The hotel is surrounded by tree-covered hills and mountains and sits next to a river. We had an excellent lunch there. Following lunch, we continued the drive with lots of other cars, trucks, and buses.

Upon arrival in the city, we checked into the Kaze Darbar hotel, where we had stayed the first nights in Kathmandu. This time I got a spacious suite with single and double beds and bathtub. That night we had dinner on the third floor of the Wellness Organic restaurant with seating on a balcony with great views of half of Kathmandu and a sliver of the moon. Emily had recovered from her sickness, so she and Bob joined us. After dinner, we went inside to watch a wonderful dance performance. It was a great ending to a wonderful trip.

By the way, on the travels around Nepal, BJ had a deck of cards, so I taught Sandy and BJ how to play "Crazy Eight." Every chance they got, they played the game, even in the back of the car as I was riding shotgun (front seat on the left side of car since the Nepalese drive on roads like the Indians and British).

We also exchanged jokes. Of course, I told all my favorite jokes. BJ and Sandy said several times that I am a real joker and said a lot of funny things and jokes.

BJ had a good one that is as follows:

Three guys—a dentist, a chemist, and a lawyer—are stranded in the Sahara Desert for many days without food or water. God answers their prayers and joins them. They each go to God one at a time. God told the dentist he could have three wishes. The dentist says he wants water, food, and to be sent home. God grants the wishes, and the dentist disappears. Next, God calls the chemist to join him. Not knowing what God granted the dentist, the chemist asks for the same three things, which are granted. The lawyer then receives God's call to join him. God tells the lawyer that he *can have three wishes. Immediately, the lawyer asks God for beer and wine. After consuming the alcohol, the lawyer asks God, "Where are my friends? I would like them to join me."*

Following breakfast on Friday morning, November 29, we were taken by taxi to Kathmandu airport, which is small with only five gates and very crowded with tourists. We had a long wait for obtaining our boarding passes to Delhi, and security and immigration were slow. There was only one café in the airport but many souvenir shops and eating places outside of security.

Upon boarding, there was another security check with the physical opening of the carry-on luggage and a pat down. We took off at 10:30 a.m. for Delhi. After landing one and a half hours later, we had a security check before going to our gate in the international terminal. It was a large and modern airport with lots of shops and restaurants. Delhi was very smoggy (known as the worst air quality of any city in the world). It was an eight-and-a-half-hour Air India flight on a Boeing 787 to Vienna. We had gained five hours.

At the Vienna airport, I said my goodbyes to Emily and Bob and took the airport nonstop underground train to the end station then the underground U-3 to the West Bohnhoff, followed by a two-block walk in the cold rain to the Michelangelo Hotel, where I had stayed on my last trip to Vienna.

It was still cold but with blue skies on Saturday. I took several streetcar trips to see my old neighborhood in the tenth district, Neustift am Walde, the house at 180 Krottenbachstrasse, as well as walks around the inner ring and the Graben and Kartnerstrasse. There was a large Kriskindlmarkt in front of the town hall that included ice-skating and a variety of amusement rides. Many tourist groups were there as well as in the inner city, the worst I had ever seen.

On Sunday, I caught the 8:00 a.m. train to Gratz to view the scenery. I had a beautiful young girl in my cabin that lived in Vienna on weekends and attended the university in Gratz during the week studying music. Although we got off in Gratz, the train continued to Ljubljana. After a short walk to see the Kriskindlmarkt, I caught the train back to Vienna. On the way back, I got a good picture of the ski area at Simmering. There was not much snow there, but they were in the process of artificially making it. The view brought back a lot of wonderful memories of skiing there with my family when we lived in Vienna. After arriving back at the main train station in Vienna, I took Tram 8 to the west train station and a short walk to the hotel. Later, I returned to Kartnerstrasse and met Ann and Courtney for schnitzel dinner at Lugeck—a branch of Figlmuller.

On Monday, December second, I met Jan at UNO City for lunch after exchanging $1,000 for 891 euros at his bank. It was good to see Jan and to hear of his recent activities. On one of my walks later in the city, I went inside the Grand Hotel that was IAEA headquarters until it was moved to UNO City in 1980. There was a shopping mall next to the hotel with lots of Kriskindlmarkt booths.

The next day, I checked out of the hotel and went to the main train station to catch the 8:00 a.m. train to Prague. It was cold that morning with gray skies and a few snowflakes. I spent the four-hour trip in the dining car eating and drinking. Upon my arrival in Prague, I took a taxi to the K&K Hotel Central. The skies were now blue and weather not so cold. I exchanged $100 for 2,250 Czech koruna at a shop near the train station. At the station, I would have received only 1,800 koruna if I would have changed money there. The next day, I got a three-day tram pass and spent some time riding the trams as well as having several walkabouts in the old town. In the town square were *many Kriskindlmarkt stalls and tourists (not as many as in Vienna but worse than I had ever seen).*

On Thursday, December 5, I took the train to Dresden. Skies went from blue to gray during the ride, but it was warmer than Prague. After my arrival, I had a walk from the train station to the river and back. There were several areas in the city center with outdoor Kriskindlmarkt stalls. Again, lots of tourists were there. Later in the day, I returned to Vienna via Prague.

After spending the night at the Airport Ibis hotel, I left Vienna for Istanbul on a Turkish Airlines flight at seven. After a four-and-a-half-hour wait in Istanbul, I caught a Turkish Airlines flight to Toronto, arriving eleven hours later. There, I stayed at the BW Plus Hotel near the airport. Early the next morning, Sunday, December 8, I took a four-hour Air Canada flight to Denver, arriving at ten.

Chapter 2
Activities in Colorado

I

James and Lara leave their office early on Friday afternoon, do some grocery shopping, and drive to Pine Shadows. As John is bringing in Lara's luggage and food into her apartment, she starts touring her new home. "John, the furniture is perfect in all the rooms." She then walks over and gives him a hug. "Thank you for providing such a wonderful place for me to live this year."

"Well, if you need anything, just call, and I will walk a mile, ha ha, to assist you. I need to run some errands now. I think you have enough food for dinner."

"Please come by when you are finished and have dinner with me. Then you can see how good Russian food cooked by me tastes."

On Saturday morning, John and Lara travel to Eric and Sylvia's home in South Boulder. Since the foursome had late breakfasts, they go directly to the Wildlife Animal Sanctuary.

After their visit to see all the wonderful animals at the sanctuary and a short walk in Downtown Denver, they return to Eric and Sylvia's home for dinner. Amy, Dave, and Lorrie arrive, and the five young adults spend most of the time exchanging information with Lara over a wonderful meal that Sylvia had prepared. There is also a discussion of everyone's activities since the young adults came to Pendleton for Ying's memorial. James asks Lara to tell the group more about her life. Next, Eric explains about his job working for a biotech company in nearby Longmont and how he and Sylvia met. "My wonderful wife works at the same company I do, and we met at CU. We bought this house last year after we were secretly married. Sorry you all were not invited to the ceremony, but it was only us, a preacher, and two of our mutual friends. We know the house is small with only two bedrooms, but housing is expensive in South Boulder, and this is all we could afford. I do plan on finishing the basement sometime in the future. Before the home purchase, we were living in separate condos and, before that, in dorm rooms at CU, finishing our doctorate's degrees, mine in organic chemistry and Sylvia's in biochemistry."

James tells Lara, "Because of their secret wedding, I had to find out about it in an e-mail from Eric. Of course, I sent them a congratulations card with a generous check."

Amy speaks up next. "After graduating from the American International School in Vienna, I returned to Colorado and started working for an investment company in Downtown Denver. There, I met Dave, who worked in a separate department for the same company. After a year of courtship, we were married and purchased a home in Aurora. Okay, Lorrie, what do you have to say?"

"Thank you, Amy. I am a senior at CU and planning to go to graduate school, majoring in organic chemistry. I am uncertain if I will continue at CU or go to another university. As you can guess, my father was a big influence on Eric and my studies. I have been staying in a student dorm."

After dinner, John and Lara thank their hosts for a wonderful day and return to Pine Shadows.

After Sunday morning breakfast, John takes Lara to Eldora for her to try some snow skiing. She is excited about learning how to ski. After John rents some skis for Lara, he shows her the basics of skiing before they take the lift to the top of the beginner's slope. Lara slowly skis next to John and makes it downhill with only one fall. They continue this routine several more times with no more falls.

After the good time skiing, they go for an early dinner at the Black Forest restaurant in Nederland. John tells Lara that it is his favorite Nederland restaurant since they have excellent Wiener schnitzel and Bratwurst. "My other favorites are Back Country Pizza, Kathmandu Restaurant, and Neds Restaurant. I usually do my grocery shopping in Boulder, but there is a nice supermarket in Nederland called B&F Supermarket. Years ago, Margrit and I have stayed at the Boulder Creek Lodge a couple of times."

"Thank you so much for taking me to the slopes and teaching me how to ski. I have really enjoyed the day and have fallen in love with the sport. I look forward to more of the same."

"I am so happy you like skiing as I think it makes winter go by faster. Maybe next weekend we can go to Breckenridge to ski. As you saw, I have my own skis. I also have a snowboard that I usually use on the slopes. Maybe after a few more trips to the slopes, you can try snowboarding. I also like to cross-country ski on the trails around Pine Shadows, but if you join me for that, you will need to buy your own skis."

After they return home, Lara gives John a thank-you with a hug. John says, "I will see you in the morning about eight so you can ride with me to the office. Now I need to do my chores around the garage and apartment. Good night."

At the staff meeting the next day, Lara tells the faculty about her planned research on treating mine water using some unique methods. John gives a summary of his student's research and announces that he was successful on one of his proposals to the National Science Foundation. Other proposals with the DOE and the Environmental Protection Agency are pending. He also informs the faculty that his students will accompany him and Lara to the Actinide Separations Conference in March.

After John and Lara arrive back at Pine Shadows in the early evening, John tells Lara, "Remember, I will take you to the Nederland bus station at seven forty-five so you can catch the eight o'clock bus to Boulder. You can phone me when you arrive back to Nederland in the late afternoon. Sometime this week, I will take you to get your driver's license so you can start driving

Whit to the bus stop or just drive directly to the office if the roads are not icy."

"What are your plans for tomorrow?"

"I will work on my chemistry textbook in the morning, followed by doing some cross-country skiing on the trail next to Pine Shadows, even though the snow is starting to disappear."

John and Lara spend most of Wednesday in the laboratory with their students, and Thursday's activities are about the same as they were on Tuesday except for John helping Lara get her driver's license. She also receives a small package at CU from Moscow containing a shot-size plastic bottle of Russian Standard Vodka made in St. Petersburg. There is no return address on the package, and she is surprised that the seal on the bottle cap is off. Lara assumes it is from her folks or brother and send them thank-you e-mails.

Following Lara's excellent seminar talk on Friday afternoon, John tells Lara in their office, "Your talk was very interesting, and you did an outstanding job in telling everyone about you work in Moscow and your planned research. Your use of the English language is first class."

"Thank you. I do enjoy my research here and your wonderful company."

"Would you be interested in seeing the eastern part of the Rocky Mountain National Park and Estes Park tomorrow?"

"Certainly. That sounds great."

"Since the highest continuous paved mountain road in the U.S. is closed for the winter, we can only drive through part of the eastern side of the park. Be sure and wear a heavy coat and bring along a hat and gloves. After the park visit, we can go into Estes Park and have lunch at the Stanley Hotel. Following our meal, we can take a walk around the interesting tourist town and then head back to Nederland. If you agree, we can go skiing on Sunday in Breckenridge."

"That sounds like a wonderful weekend."

"Although Randy uses a snowblower to clear the driveway after snowstorms, he usually does not clear the tennis court. An exception was the time I had an open house party after I moved into my apartment. When the snow disappears in the early spring, I will teach you how to play tennis. Maybe when the Boulder Golf Club opens, we can play some golf. I am impressed that you are so good at playing pool, and I do love playing chess with you despite losing about half of the games we have played. Before we drive to San Diego next month, I would like to show you on the weekends some of the places on the northern front range, such as Colorado State University in Fort Collins and maybe even Cheyenne, Wyoming. We can visit Garden of the Gods, Pike's Peak, Colorado Springs, and Pueblo on our trip to San Diego. On our return from California, we can stop at Grand Junction, Glenwood Springs, Aspen, and Vail."

"By the way, John, last night I read about your trip to Lebanon and Kurdistan, and it was fascinating reading. I really enjoyed reading about such faraway places that I will probably never get to visit."

"Some of the details in my diary of the places I visited in Lebanon and Kurdistan were taken from an excellent brochure of Spiekermann Travel Service."

My British Air flight left DIA at 7:30 p.m. for London. I lucked out as I got a whole middle row of four seats. However, I got little sleep. I did watch a good movie as well as beat the plane's computer at chess, three games out of five. The flight to London in the Boeing 747 was nine hours. At Heathrow, as I waited for my British Air flight to Beirut, I met one of my tour travelers, Diana Brown. She is a widow about sixty and lives on a small farm, a two-hour drive from Charlotte, North Carolina. She has her house for sale as she plans to move to Texas to be near her two sons.

Following the five-hour flight, immigration (visa on arrival), and customs, I exchanged some dollars for the *local currency (100 livres for $0.75), even though everyone uses U.S. dollars in Lebanon. We were met by a driver from the local tour operator. The ride to the nice Arjaan Hotel was about twenty minutes. The hotel has seventeen floors and a swimming pool on the roof, two restaurants, a business center, and meeting rooms downstairs. I got a spacious room on the eighth floor. The room overlooks some beautiful rock formations (called Pigeon) near the shore of the Mediterranean Sea. There is a large Starbucks across the street that borders the sea and has an open-air seating area so the patrons can enjoy the sea view. Next to the hotel is a KFC, and a block down the street is a Pizza Hut.*

On Wednesday morning, I went down for a wonderful breakfast that had a large variety of food to eat. During breakfast, about two hundred soldiers carrying AK-47s marched by outside. There were also lots of young slim girls jogging past the hotel. Following breakfast, I took a couple of walks along the seashore, a nap, got caught up on this diary, and worked on my general chemistry book.

On the walk by the sea, there were piles of trash, mainly plastic bottles, everywhere. Taxis would come by slowly and honk their horn, wanting me to ride—very annoying. I did not like hearing all the honking I heard in the room either. In the evening, I had a nice buffet dinner and got to meet more of my traveling companions.

In the morning, there was also an excellent buffet breakfast. At eight, my fellow passengers and I boarded a bus. Our guide was Pauline from the Tourism Company. We also had an expert on Lebanese culture and the history of the country. Bruce was from the UK and gave us background information on our way to the first stop. Part of what Bruce stated was that Beirut stands on the site of a very ancient settlement going back at least five thousand years. Its name appeared in the Cuneiform Inscriptions as early as the fourteenth century BC. Berytus, as it was called then, became a Roman colony under Roman rule and was the seat of a famous law school, which continued into the Byzantine. In the following century, Arab Muslim forces took the city, and in 1110, it fell to the Crusaders. Beirut remained in Crusaders' hands until 1291, when it was conquered by the Mamlukes. Ottoman rule began in 1516 and continued for four hundred years until the defeat of the Turks in World War I. The French Mandate period followed, and in 1943, Lebanon gained its independence.

On the drive south, there were many big and beautiful homes on the hills and mountainsides, some under construction. All the homes going up had concrete pillars with cinder block walls. The floor and roofs were concrete. Some homes looked like mansions. There were also many farms growing bananas and olives. We went through several small towns, and a few of them had a KFC, McDonald's, Pizza Hut, and Burger King.

After about an hour's drive, we visited the town of Mleeta to see the Hezbollah Resistance Museum. It is an open-air war museum created by the Islamic militant organization Hezbollah to commemorate the battles they fought against the Israeli troops in and around the site of the museum. There were many guns and helmets on the ground, and a couple of tanks were also displayed.

Next, we took a drive to Saida, where we had a spectacular lunch at a restaurant next to the Sea Castle that sits in the sea. Following lunch, we had a short walk near the castle and through a bazaar.

After the visit to Saida and about an hour's drive, we arrived in Tyre, where we visited the ruins at the sanctuary and the Hippodrome. Most signs are both in Arabic and English, and so far, all the vendors took U.S. dollars. On the way back to Beirut, we had a short stop at Eshmun, a Phoenician site in Lebanon, followed by another stop in

Maghdouché to see the castle and the Al-Saydeh ancient church.

In Beirut, we had a short visit to the Soap Museum. This thematic museum is an old soap factory where basins date back to the seventeenth century. Visitors can have a look at the different stages of the manufacturing of artisanal olive oil soap using traditional instruments and tools. Window cases also display traditional items used in hammams as well as pipes and pottery found on the site.

There were a couple of good rainstorms in the afternoon, but when it rained, we were lucky to be either in the restaurant or on the bus. In the evening, we went to the Bay Rock restaurant across from the hotel. Many different dishes of food were brought to the table. I sat across the table from Bill and Helen, who run a travel agency in Chicago. Their good friend Phyllis also was on the trip. It was interesting that there were two medical doctors, a nurse, and two lawyers in the group.

After a nice buffet breakfast on Friday, October 26, we went south again but this time on a highway near the top of the mountains, where we had a great view of the sea and house-covered hills. Our first visit was to Chouf Mountain and the village of Deir El Qamar that has the historic residence of the governors of Lebanon. We then continued to Beit ed-Dine, where a superb palace stands over the valley with its typical Lebanese architecture of the eighteenth and nineteenth century. We visited the museum containing a unique exhibition of mosaics. Next, we proceeded to the Moussa Castle, an interesting place since it was built by only one person in devotion to a promised wife. After lunch in a local restaurant in Beit ed-Dine, we visited the Druze leader Mr. Joumblat Walid in his residence in Moukhtara (he had a Mercedes-Benz once owned by Hitler), followed by a visit to Maasser el Chouf, Arc En Ciel.

On Saturday, we headed north, along with hundreds of other cars, to Tripoli. Near Tripoli, we headed east to the mountains. On the way, we went past a small castle near a reservoir under construction. From there, we saw snowcapped mountains near the Cedars (an area of cedar trees aging more than two thousand years of which only about four hundred remain) and a nearby ski area. We stopped for coffee and WCs at Kousba, where our group had a nice walk through the cedar forest, which is today an ecomuseum. The group had lunch at the Saba near the Cedars. Afterward, we continued to Bsharri, a village in the Kadisha Valley and hometown of the Lebanese poet Kahlil Gibran. Bsharri and nearby Kozhaya are famous for their magnificent, excellently preserved sites such as the Gibran Museum and the Monastery of St. Anthony. That evening, dinner was at the hotel restaurant.

The clocks fell back an hour on Sunday, just like in the U.S. I commented how Lebanon is so much like the U.S. It seemed like everyone speaks English, dresses like Americans, there are many American cars on the roads, and Christians and Muslims work together; all American fast-food restaurants, including Dunkin Donuts, are here. I was informed that there are some public buses but no light rail, trains, or subways. The highways are full of traffic.

After breakfast, we drove by Pigeons Rock on Coastal Avenue to the city center, where one of the largest reconstruction projects in the world took place. We also visited the National Museum. The museum opened in 1942 to house Lebanon's archeological treasure and has been a landmark both in times of peace and turmoil. During the war, when the museum stood on the dangerous "green line" that divided Beirut, the antiquities it housed were removed for safekeeping. Larger objects were covered with concrete to ensure their protection. From prehistoric flint tools and weapons to Greco-Roman objects and large collections from

Byblos, the museum's holdings reflect Lebanon's national heritage. The museum has been fully restored. The city tour ended in Nejmeh Square with a tower clock, surrounded by the Lebanese Parliament, two churches, and three other impressive buildings.

Our travels continued out of the city along the Dog River to the Jeita Grotto. The grotto is in the valley of Nahr al-Kalb, about ten miles north of Beirut. The grotto was discovered in 1836 by an American missionary, who, venturing some 150 feet into the cave, fired a shot from a gun and found a cavern of major importance. The grotto was formed during the past thousand years and continues to grow by very frequent drops of water that mold the stalactites on the ceiling and the stalagmites on the floor of the galleries and halls. The Jeita Grotto is characterized by its unique, dazzling beauty and the most varied shaped, sized, and colored limestone formations.

The lower gallery was opened to the public in 1958 and is where our group took a short dreamy cruise in a rowboat around about 1,200 feet of the cave's total length of 23,400 feet.

Our group then had a walk in the upper gallery that was inaugurated in 1969. We got to discover extraordinary stone forms of curtains, columns, draperies, and mushrooms. One of the longest stalactites in the world measuring 25 feet is in the upper grotto. The distance from the ceiling to the level of water reaches over 300 feet. There is a small chapel in a large short cave near the grotto. At the chapel, we got to witness the baptism of a small beautiful girl. According to legend, going into this cave makes one crazy. I think my visit there made me lose my craziness.

After lunch, we proceed to Harissa via the coastal highway. There, we went by cable car to the Holy Statue of Notre Dame for a great view of Beirut to the south and the small city of Jounieh to the north.

The bus continued on the northern coast to Byblos, the oldest town in the world continuously inhabited for the last five thousand years. There, we visited the Citadel, St. John's Church, and the harbor. The Citadel is a large Crusader land castle near the present port area. Excavations in 1995 revealed a large well-preserved section of the foundation wall complete with Roman column drums used as bond stones or reinforcement.

Our final stop was at the Mosul Nabu Museum near Sandy beach on the Mediterranean Sea. It is named after the Mesopotamian patron gold of literacy. The museum offers an exceptional permanent collection of early Bronze and Iron Age artifacts; antiquities from the Roman, Greek, Byzantine, and Muslim epochs; rare manuscripts; and ethnographic material. The museum's collection also includes examples of local and regional modern art by key artists. Notable in Nabu's collection is a unique selection of Sumerian and Babylonian cuneiform tablets and Phoenician steles dating from 2330 to 540 BCE that recount epic tales, give indications of economic systems, information on ethnic groups, and maps of ancient cities. The collection also holds an extensive collection of nineteenth- and early twentieth-century photographs and postcards. The museum houses a library with books on art, archeology, history, geography, travels, and a collection of rare manuscripts.

On Monday, we went across Mount Lebanon and then descended toward the Beqaa Valley to reach the world's greatest historical site. In Baalbek, we first stopped at a quarry that has a thousand-ton monolith, which the Romans had destined to be part of the podium of the Jupiter Temple, but the temple was never completed, and the monolith remained in the quarry. Next, we went to the Baalbek temple ruins. The group also spent some time touring the Temple of Jupiter and Bacchus.

We had lunch at Monte Alberto, an Armenian restaurant in the town of Zahlé. The son of the owner spent three years in Memphis, Tennessee, and then returned to Lebanon so his two daughters could learn English better as well as Arabic and French in school. He plans on going back to the U.S. in a few years.

Following lunch, we made a stop at the Château Ksara for some wine tasting and a tour of the production facilities and cellars, where the wine is aged in barrels from France. The château is nestled between two large mountains within the fertile Beqaa Valley. The average elevation is three thousand feet. The Beqaa has a Mediterranean climate and its own water table because of melted snow from the mountains. Château Ksara, the country's oldest winery, was established in 1857, when Jesuit fathers inherited the estate and began farming a sixty-seven-acre plot of land to produce Lebanon's first nonsweet red wine. The Jesuit monks accidentally discovered a grotto stretching over more than a mile that gave them the perfect storage area for the wine. It was dug in limestone rock and is believed that the grotto dates to the Roman period. In 1973, the Vatican encouraged its monasteries and missions around the world to sell off any commercial activities. By then, the winery was optioned to a consortium of Lebanese businessmen. Three million bottles of wine are now produced each year from three thousand tons of grapes.

After the château visit, we proceeded to Anjar, the only Umayyad site in Lebanon and recognized to be one of the major marketplaces on the Silk Road. We also visited the farms of Taanayel.

That evening, we had a nice dinner at a restaurant across from the hotel and next to Starbucks. After dinner, we said our goodbyes to our guide as well as the others who were not going on to Iraq the next day.

On Tuesday, October 30, we were bused to the Beirut airport. The airport is nice with twenty-one gates and many shops and restaurants. Our Middle East Airlines flight left Beirut at two and arrived in Erbil, Kurdistan, at five. We had changed to another time zone and lost an hour. After the group collected their luggage (I was the only one that did not check in a suitcase), we had a short wait to get through immigration. The agent was very friendly. He said the visa that I received was good for thirty days. I did not exchange any money as U.S. dollars are accepted everywhere; I did get a little of the local currency later, 1,200 livres for $1. We then had to catch a bus to an outside arrival area, where our host met us and took us by bus to the Van Royal Hotel. The hotel is nice but not quite a five star as claimed. The group and I had an excellent dinner—a great salad and mixed grill (beef, chicken, and fish) and a variety of desserts. After dinner, I found out that the TV in my room has over a hundred channels to choose from.

On Halloween morning, we had a fantastic buffet breakfast with many things to choose from. At nine thirty, the bus picked us up for visits to various places in Erbil. Our guide was Balin, and the expert was Doug, an elderly American who had spent a good deal of his adult life traveling in the Middle East. He had written a book on Kurdistan and does artwork, mainly restoring antique jewelry. He also wrote a book about Willy Bozan, whom he personally knew.

Erbil is about 210 miles southeast of Mosul and 60 miles northwest of Slemani. It is the oldest continuously inhabited city in the world. (There are cities as old but not continuously inhabited.) Its name was mentioned in the historic writings around the year 3000 BC as the name of a town full of life, which was a Sumerian property. According to the Sumerian writings, the name of the town at the time was Urbiliom in one of the writings of the Sumerian king (Shulgi) around 200 BC. The golden ages of Erbil were the Neo-Assyrian period circa 1000–612 BC, the capital of the kingdom of Adiabene, first century BC–First century AD, the reign of Musaffer Ed-Din Kokburi, AD 1190–1232, and the capital of the autonomous Kurdistan Region of Iraq since 2005.

After a drive around the city, we took about a twenty-mile ride north to the town of Shaqlawa. Known as the Pride of Kurdistan, Shaqlawa is a popular holiday destination because it has an abundance of waterfalls, springs, trees, and greeneries. Its beautiful nature and climate attract tourists from across Iraq and abroad most weekends, and by dusk, the streets are full of visitors strolling through the peaceful streets, window-shopping, snacking from street vendors, and enjoying one of the town's many restaurants. Most of the population of Shaqlawa are Kurds and Assyrians who belong to the Chaldean Church. So traditionally, the city has a multicultural, peaceful, tolerant society and is friendly toward foreigners. Our group took a long walk up a mountain via more than a thousand concrete steps to the ancient shrine of Raban Boya (Sheikh Wso Rahman). There, everyone enjoyed a wonderful view of the Safeen Mountain valley in the opposite direction of Shaqlawa. The shrine is popular among religious pilgrims. There is a large smooth boulder there where, according to legend, if a woman is infertile and slides down the rock on her back headfirst, she will be cured and can then have children (that is if she survives the slide). Later, we had lunch, followed by a town walk for shopping. We returned to the hotel about three for a rest. We had dinner at a classy restaurant outside the hotel.

On Thursday, the first of November, we started our day touring the seven-thousand-year-old Citadel of Erbil. The citadel is considered among the most ancient citadels known to the world. It was built in the center of Erbil City on a seventy-five-foot hill. The citadel covers a large area, and its construction dates to 6,000 BC. The number of dwellings inside the citadel amounts to 506. It is divided into three quarters: Al Saray, Topkhana, and Takyah.

The archaeological mound of the Erbil Citadel, which is seventy-five feet high at its highest point, is the result of the natural accumulation of the remains of successive civilizations over a history of at least six thousand years. The earliest evidence of occupation is in the Ubaid period, the first period in history when many people started to live in towns. Throughout history, the high mound was a notable landmark on the ancient "Royal Road" or for travelers crossing the Zagros from the east.

The first mention of Erbil is in two clay tablets from Ebla in Syria, which mention a messenger traveling there around 2300 BC. About one hundred years later, other records describe the capture of the governor in the mountains nearby, and in circa 2100 BC, there are many Sumerian texts recording Erbil's incorporation into the third empire of Ur. Erbil soon became independent again and by 1716 BC was probably the religious capital of the kingdom of Qabra, which in that year became part of the first Assyrian Empire of Shamshi-Adad I. For nearly a thousand years ending in 612 BC, Erbil was one of the main cities in the Assyrian Empire, famous for the temple of Ishtar in the citadel. The temple housed a scribal school, an astronomical observatory, and priestesses who foretold the future. It may have gone out of use when the Assyrian Empire was destroyed by a coalition of Babylonians and Medes, the possible ancestors of the Kurds, who gained possession of Erbil at that time.

Darius I unified the administration of the succeeding Achaemenid Empire in 521 BC and executed a local leader in Erbil who claimed descent from Median royalty. Darius III chose Erbil as his base in 331 BC before he faced defeat by Alexander the Great at the nearby Battle of Gaugamela (or Arbela). After the battle, Alexander found Darius's treasure and royal clothes abandoned in the citadel. Following

Alexander's premature death, his brother became governor of Erbil in 321 BC.

The Greek-speaking Seleucid Empire conquered by the Parthians, who allowed Erbil autonomous status as the capital of the kingdom of Adiabene (Hedyab), which was prominent in the first century BC and first century AD, became a center of Judaism and was later the seat of a Christian archbishop. Adiabene often became a battleground between the Parthian/Sassanian and Roman/Byzantine empires, particularly in the key periods of conflict—AD 116–118, 195, 216 (when the royal tombs at Erbil were destroyed), 354, and 627.

The Umayyads developed Mosul as the provincial capital, and Erbil temporarily lost its importance, but this returned when Zengi captured the citadel in 1126 or 1128. After 1190, when Sultan Muzaffer Ed-Din Kokburi became ruler, Erbil was the capital of an emirate, which occupied much of Northern Iraq, and the city became a noted center of culture and learning during the late Abbasid period. Not long after the death of Muzaffer Ed-Din in 1232, the Mongols devastated the lower city, although they failed to capture the citadel, finally acquiring it by negotiation following the siege of 1258/1259.

After Erbil emerged as an important staging post on the route between Mongol domains in Iraq and Persia and Central Asia and China, it became part of the Black Sheep and White Sheep domains. Between 1508 and 1535, it formed part of the Safavid Empire, when its transfer to Ottoman rule was accomplished without violence.

In 1743, the citadel was besieged for sixty days by Nader Shah, the ruler of Persia, during which the city walls were severely damaged. In 1745, the Ottoman Sultan Murad I ordered that the defenses should be surveyed and repaired, but it seems that only the Grand Gate was reconstructed, and the remainder of the defensive circuit was replaced by the present perimeter of houses. Even without city walls, the citadel was difficult to capture, and in 1835, the garrison of the prince of Soran was besieged in the citadel by Ottoman troops.

In 1918, a British administration took control of Erbil. After Iraqi Independence in 1932, the establishment of peace and security encouraged the wealthier inhabitants to abandon the citadel in favor of new houses in the lower town, and the citadel started to fall into decay.

A new wave of inhabitants came to live in the citadel from 1986 onward in the form of refugees fleeing the destruction of their villages by the previous Iraqi regime. In 2006, the KRG decided that they had to be relocated so that the citadel could be restored and revitalized. A massive restoration project is currently being undertaken by UNESCO.

After our group wondered around the citadel, we had a tour of the famous Textile Museum in the citadel. Women are taught on site how to weave in traditional style with the goal of preserving the ancient arts of the land. The fascinating art of felt making is also practiced on site. We also visited the Citadel Museum that is housed in a 220-year-old residence. It features ancient Kurdish fighting tools, traditional dresses, handmade rugs from different regions and eras of Kurdish history, jewelry, and photos. In addition to Kurdish antiquities, there are several pieces from Iran and Turkey as well as some photos of important people who had visited the citadel; one showed a visit by Senators John McCain and Lindsey Graham. At the museum's gift shop, we had an opportunity to acquire a sample of local crafts. Across from the museum is a large and well-known antique shop where one could acquire a piece of Kurdistan's history as well as its more modern crafts. Our last stop was at the local bazaar (Qaysari), where one can find jewelry, carpets, and souvenirs. Later, we returned to the hotel for dinner.

On Friday, November second, we left the city and headed toward Mosul. The highway was not good in a lot of places, mainly because of all the semitrucks, many hauling petroleum from the many oil wells in the area. On the way, we passed many hills of trees that our guide said had been planted. Our first stop was at the Dayro d-Mor Mattai Monastery, about sixty miles from Erbil. The monastery is one of the eastern Christendom's most famous sites and apart from a few forced closures has been in continuous use for nearly two thousand years. St. Matthew founded the monastery in the third century BC and is buried there. We had a tour conducted by one of the monastery's monks.

Later, we departed the monastery for Gaugamela, site of the famous battle between King Darius III and Alexander the Great. While standing on a hill overlooking the vast plain below, we received a lecture from Doug about the battle that made Alexander king of Persia, an undisputed ruler of the civilized world.

After lunch, we went to see Jirwan, the oldest aqueduct and bridge ruin in the world built in the time of Sennacherib (690 BC). The site was once part of a vast complex that was built to water the Gardens of Nineveh. Huge stones were transported by hand from quarries hundreds of miles away and are scripted with the story of this amazing feat. The "hidden message of Sennacherib" is there.

Next, we visited Lalish, pilgrimage site of the Yezidis, who are descendants of the Zoroastrians—one of the most mysterious people in the world. Doug told us about the ancient rituals of these people that are considered by many to be the remnant of the original religion of Kurdistan. From there, we departed for Duhok and took up residency at the wonderful Rixos Hotel.

Bill and I joked a lot and were always goofing off. One evening after dinner, Bill told me that the Kurds are a very friendly and polite people. "I heard that they are so friendly that if two of them want the same thing when they are shopping together, it takes a little time for each of them to say 'No, you take it.' The joke I heard was about two Kurds with guns who wanted to shoot each other. Again, it took some time for each Kurd to say several times 'No, you go ahead and shoot first.'"

After a great buffet breakfast in the main dining room of the Rixos, we departed Duhok for Amadiya, an ancient city dating back at least to the Assyrian era. Located on the high promontory above a breathtaking landscape and fed by a geothermal spring originating far below the mountain, it was once an almost impenetrable fortress. The city gate (Bab Zebar), located in the eastern side of the city, was built in AD 500–600. There is also a third-century synagogue in this once important Jewish city. Amadiya was also a center of Chaldean astrology and astronomy, and local tradition holds that the Magi of Christmas fame began their journey here.

After lunch, we departed for Rawanduz through breathtaking scenery in the region of Barzan, where we met a local official and saw the Mala Mustafa Memorial (father of modern Kurdistan).

Next, we continued our journey by going through Soran and passing by Shanidar Cave, where some of the world's most important prehistoric remains were discovered. Shanidar Cave contained about sixty skeletons dating back eighty thousand years and was home to history's most famous Neanderthal—"Nandy." The cave is located on the Bradost Mountain within the borders of the Mergasoor district. It is well-known for its distinct triangular shape and sits at an altitude of 6,600 feet above sea level with a height of 54 feet and a depth of 120 feet. It is one of the largest and most ancient caves in Iraq, dating back to 60,000 years BC. The cave was used during the revolution times as a hideout for the Peshmerga. Excavations were first enacted in 1951 by Mr. Rafsolki, an archaeologist who analyzed the stone layers and managed to pinpoint the age.

We finished the day by going up a high mountain winding road to the top of Bradost Mountain, seventy-two miles north of Erbil. The mountain is 2,300 feet above sea level. The road was built by Saddam Hussein's workers years ago to travel to an observatory. It was a thirty-minute ride to the top, where the Pank Resort Hotel is located. The resort has over forty bungalows, each with four suites (separate bedroom, bathroom, kitchen, and living room). It also has a large dining room, play area outside, ski area, and ski lift to bring skiers from the other side of the mounatin.

The next morning, we went back on the same scary road on our way to Sulaymaniyah. I was sitting in the death seat, and the driver drove too fast and followed too close to the car/truck in front of us. The drive continued to a four-lane highway that paralleled the Zab River in the Ali Begg Valley that dips between the Korek and Bradost mountains. It is seven miles long with many beautiful sites such as springs and waterfalls. The famed Gali waterfall is in this valley, which is a popular site for tourists from all around the country to visit. There are also several restaurants and cafés in the valley built to accommodate visitors. We stopped in this area to have a one-mile walk on part of the Hamilton Road that was built in 1928 to 1932.

We then continued our drive to Sulaymaniyah via beautiful Lake Dukan and had lunch at Kosrat Restaurant in Dukan. Everyone enjoyed the local cuisine that included fresh fish from nearby lakes and streams.

In the late afternoon, we visited the Red House (Amna Suraka), the site of many atrocities committed by Saddam Hussein at the former intelligence headquarters and jail. The building consists of two floors. Each floor has four spacious halls. They were all previously used as dormitories for the security staff. The first hall of the first floor is now used as a museum/exhibition of the great exodus of 1991. The secondary halls of both floors are now functioning as cinemas to show documentary films and places for artistic activities. The first hall on the second floor is used to show the different types of land mines that have been planted in Kurdistan as well as the bombs used by different artilleries.

The corridor on the first floor, which was used by the officers to have access to the rooms, was turned into a symbol of Anfal operations and the destroyed villages perpetrated by the regime. The 182,000 pieces of broken mirror fixed to the wall symbolize the number of the victims exterminated during the Anfal campaign, while the 4,500 small electrical light bulbs symbolize the number of Kurdish villages destroyed by the now overthrown regime. The frontal section of the building used to be a restaurant and a cafeteria for the officers but is now used as offices for the museum staff. The second floor, which has meeting halls, has now been turned into a national library.

During Ba'athist times, another building was a center for controlling the security operations performed to watch the activities of the citizens and monitor publications issued in Sulaymaniyah. The building saw an active role in working to erase the Kurdish national identity and to distort their culture, not to forget that the main duty of this horrifying fort was torturing and killing the inhabitants of the city and of the entire Sulaymaniyah governorate. The first floor was a center for interrogating detainees. Parallel to this one, two other floors were designed to keep the detainees according to various categories; men, women, and children were kept in different rooms. Moreover, there were solitary cells and torturing places, which are kept the way they were.

The building was handed over in 1984 and was used to full capacity until it was liberated during the Kurdish Uprising in 1991. The place was then turned into a shelter for displaced families from Kirkuk and remained so till

1996, when Mrs. Hero Ibrahim Ahmed offered a new place for those refugees and then offered to pay the expenses of turning the entire place into a national museum.

Following the depressing visit to the museum, we checked into the wonderful Millennium Hotel. Before dinner, we had a visit to the local bazaar for some shopping.

On Monday, I decided to stay and relax at the hotel. There, I did some writing, had a walk, took a nap, watched some television, and got a massage by a young lady from Bali. I did have breakfast and dinner with my group. Over dinner, I found out that I did not miss too much on the day's activities. They had visited the Museum of Antiquities and viewed Kurdistan's largest collection of artifacts dating back thousands of years. The group also went to Halabja, where on March 16, 1988, Saddam Hussein ordered the use of chemical weapons in attacking twenty-four villages in the Kurdish region begging with Halabja. At least five thousand people died as an immediate result of the chemical attack, and it is estimated that a further ten thousand people were injured or suffered long-term illness. Before the war ended, the Iraqis moved in on the ground and destroyed the town. In March 2010, the Iraqi High Criminal Court recognized the Halabja massacre as genocide. Saddam was executed for other crimes just before he was to be tried in Kurdistan for his acts of atrocity. Today the city lives again—testimony to the Kurds' amazing resilience and ability to survive the most brutal assault on their people and culture.

On our last day of touring, we departed for Erbil, stopping en route at the prehistoric Qizqipan Cave (village of Zarzi). Then we continued to the old Jewish city of Koy Sanjaq (Koya). There, we visited an old Jewish house and caravanserai (hostel on the ancient Silk Road) and took photos from a vantage point with views for hundreds of miles in each direction. Following our arrival in Erbil, we checked into Van Royal Hotel. We then went to our guide's nice home for snacks, coffee, and tea and met his wife and two boys. During the war, our guide went to London to work. There, he met his wife.

In general, it was a great week of tours, from one end of Kurdistan to the other. The weather had been excellent, and a light rain shower one afternoon did not slow us down. On our tours, there were periodic police checkpoints, where a few times our driver had to show his driver's license. I enjoyed everyone in our group on the tour, especially Bill.

At the Erbil airport, we had to go through a security check that was unlike any I have ever experienced. About a mile from the airport, we were stopped, the bus searched, and everyone had to show their passports. Then we were dropped at the bus terminal, where we went through an airport type of security screening, i.e., X-ray of luggage and metal detection for passengers. We then boarded a bus for the terminal. There, we went through another complete airport security process. This was repeated a third time after we got our boarding passes and went through immigration. It took at least thirty minutes to get through immigration.

Most of our group were traveling to Saudi Arabia for another tour. One lady in our group, an attorney, was going to Baghdad for a tour. Our guide did not want to tell her about a recent kidnapping of a group of tourists there.

The airport is nice and new with a large duty-free shop, a couple of cafés, and two terminals, each one with six gates. Nearby is the old airport that the U.S. Air Force is now using.

My Qatar Airline flight to Frankfurt was via Doha. On the flight, the passengers got a nice lunch, and I had some fun with a boy about eight years old who was sitting behind me with his sister and mother. I made different funny faces through the space between my seat and the adjoining one that the boy returned with laugher. After arrival in Frankfurt, I overnighted at the airport hotel before boarding

my nonstop Lufthansa Airline flight to Denver. It had been
an exciting and educational trip.

II

The next day after breakfast, James and Lara visit the colorful tourist town of Estes Park, followed by a drive through the eastern part of Rocky Mountain National Park. Following their return to Nederland, Lara thanks James for the wonderful day. "I especially liked the park and seeing so many deer and mountain sheep. I had hoped we would see a bear and/or a mountain lion. I was surprised by the small herd of elk in Estes Park, and the lunch we had at the restaurant of the Stanley Hotel was exceptionally good. I did see that the hotel was the same one in the movie *The Shining*."

"There have been several bear visits to Estes Park, Nederland, and even Boulder, looking for food, mainly in trash cans. After the road through the park is cleared of snow in a few weeks, we can take a drive through the entire park and return to Nederland via Grand Lake, Granby, Winter Park that has a ski area, Idaho Springs, and Black Hawk."

Early the next morning, the couple travels to the old mining town of Breckenridge. James tells Lara on the way, "Breckenridge was founded by prospectors mining in the nearby mountains. Tourism and skiing are now the main attractions. When the kids were young, Margrit and I had many visits to Breckenridge. We had a time-share condo for the first week of each year, and I would always take Margrit and the kids to ski, ice-skate, and walk around town, looking in the many shops. We would also try to eat at different restaurants for dinner. The family and I always had breakfast at the condo and would usually have lunch at the same restaurant at the base of one of the ski lifts. Breckenridge is where Margrit and the kids learned to ski. I got my ski lessons in a gym class at the university, where my class would spend the weekends at another ski area above Georgetown, the old mining town we stopped at coming here this morning."

After a wonderful day of skiing, and during the drive back to Nederland, Lara thanks John again for taking her to Breckenridge. "The lovely old mining town is certainly interesting, especially with its original buildings, and the ski runs are great, maybe a little better than Eldora."

The following Saturday, Amy and Dave host a day early birthday party for John. Lara and the whole family, including John's elder brother, Bill, and his wife, Kay, attend the festivities. It is a fun party in Aurora, where John receives lots of gifts. Everyone enjoys the food and birthday cake as well as the family reunion. The party ends with Amy telling everyone that she is going to have a baby in about eight months. The visitors all congratulate the couple and give their thanks for a wonderful time as they slowly depart. On the drive back to Nederland, Lara asks John, "I thought you had two sisters?"

"They died of cancer several years ago and are now in heaven with my folks and relatives."

"I am so sorry, John."

The next day, Lara invites John, Randy, and Gail for an early dinner to celebrate John's birthday. Following the meal and cake, Lara asks everyone what they would like to have to drink for a toast to John. Gail and Randy say they prefer a shot glass of brandy. Lara says, "I will have the same. John, since this is a special occasion, I think you should have a Russian drink. How about a shot of vodka?"

"You know that I do not drink, but since this is my birthday, just give me half a shot glass of the vodka." After the toasts and expressions of gratitude to Lara, John returns to his apartment, and Gail and Randy go upstairs for the night.

Ten minutes later, Randy receives a frantic call from John, saying that he is extremely sick and needs his help. Randy runs over to the garage to attend to John and finds him passed out on the floor of his bathroom, with his face in a pool of vomit.

He moves John to a dry spot in the bathroom and turns him over to see if he is still breathing. After making sure he is alive, Randy immediately calls 911 and briefly tells the operator John's condition. Ten minutes later, a Nederland Fire Rescue EMS vehicle arrives. The paramedic starts to attend John. Gail and Lara had heard the siren and rush to John's side, where they ask Randy what happened. "All I know is John called me and asked for help. I came down and found him here on the floor unconscious."

John is rushed to the main Boulder hospital. Randy, along with Gail and Lara, drive to the hospital. They anxiously sit in the waiting room. About an hour later, the doctor comes in and tells the three that they have stabilized John after stopping the internal bleeding and pumping out his stomach and intestinal track. "The digestive track contents are now in the laboratory for analysis. What did John eat for dinner?"

Lara speaks up. "We all had the same food, but John had a half of shot glass of vodka while we had brandy for a birthday toast."

"Is there any vodka left so we can have it analyzed?"

"Yes, I can bring it back to you later."

"We will keep John stabilized and see what the analysis shows. Meanwhile, there is no need for you all to wait here. I will call you if things change. But please get the bottle of vodka to me as soon as possible, and on your way out, ask the nurse for a sample jar to place some of John's vomit in for analysis."

After the three returns to Pine Shadows, Randy volunteers to take the half-full bottle of vodka and sample of vomit to the doctor.

Late the next morning, Lara receives a call from the doctor. "The analysis of John's stomach and digestive track contents and the vomit and vodka shows high levels of arsenic. John is slowly recovering and should be allowed to go home tomorrow. He might not have recovered if he had drunk a full shot glass of the vodka. Where did you get the vodka?"

"It arrived about two weeks ago from Moscow, and my parents and brother wrote that they did not send it. I do not know who would have sent it, but it appears like the sender wanted to poison me."

Late the next afternoon, Lara picks up John from the hospital and takes him home. On the way, she tells John what the doctor told her about the analysis and their discussion on the origin of the vodka. "Do you think Ivan, your ex-husband, could have sent it?"

"Yes, he did try and kill me after our divorce."

After they arrive home, he thanks her for bringing him home and asks her to give his appreciation to Randy for his kind help. "I now want to spend the rest of the day and tomorrow in bed and probably the rest of the week at home. Please inform Bob of my situation when you go to campus tomorrow. We should be thankful we are having some nice weather."

As John is resting in bed, he wonders if Lara could have tried to kill him. She could have easily lied about the bottle of vodka coming from Moscow and got some arsenic from the lab to put in the vodka that she had purchased at a liquor store. *I think I will now be more careful around her in case my hunch is true. I will ask her the next time we are together if she has any relatives named Pushkin.*

John's thoughts about Lara trying to kill him were reinforced the next morning. He had had a terrible nightmare about Lara killing him in their office with a hunting knife.

That evening, Lara comes to John's apartment and asks him if he needs anything. He tells her that he will confine himself to his apartment for the rest of the week and the weekend and does not need anything.

"John, if you do not mind, I would like to read about your trip to India. I brought the book home."

"No problem. Good night."

The nonstop flight from Denver to Tokyo was twelve hours. The plane landed at Narita the next afternoon at five. After one night at the International Garden Hotel near the airport, I flew to Kolkata (Calcutta) via Nanjing and Kunming, both China Eastern flights, landing at midnight. I was met by a driver from the LaLit Great Eastern hotel, holding a sign with my name on it. The ride to the hotel took almost an hour on a four-lane highway, elevated in several areas and lit up with unique lighting, i.e., the poles were wrapped with small colored lights, and large lights were on top of the poles. The city is big and has many new apartment buildings, old buildings with remarkable architecture, and slum and shack areas in numerous places. The five-star LaLit hotel is in a white brick structure with six floors. My room is on the fifth floor, strangely in room 3503. There are two nice restaurants in the hotel as well as a spa, workout room, swimming pool, business center, and meeting rooms.

Kolkata is the capital of the Indian state of West Bengal. Located on the east bank of the Hooghly River, it is the principal commercial, cultural, and educational center of East India, while the Port of Kolkata is India's oldest operating port as well as its sole major riverine port. As of 2011, the city had 4.5 million residents; the urban agglomeration, which comprises the city and its suburbs, is home to approximately 18 million, making it the third-most populous metropolitan area in India.

After a great buffet breakfast on Monday morning, I had a walk about the area of the hotel. The hotel is a few minutes' walk to a major street that is lined with several beautiful buildings and other office and apartment buildings. On the ground floors are various shops. Across from the hotel are two old vacant buildings that once upon a time were beautiful. Nearby is a slum area with lots of trash and rubble about. At ten, Sangram, my driver/tour guide, arrived in his black Toyota sedan. He took me on a wonderful four-hour tour of this sprawling metropolis. Some of the places we saw and briefly stopped at were Victoria Memorial (a large marble building that was built between 1906 and 1921 and dedicated to the memory of Queen Victoria, 1819–1901); the Birla Planetarium (a single-storied circular structure designed in the typical Indian style, whose architecture is loosely styled on the Buddhist stupa at Sanchi. It is the largest planetarium in Asia and the second largest planetarium in the world); Mother Teresa's house; the Indian Museum (founded by the Asiatic Society of Bengal. It the largest and oldest museum in India, which has rare collections of antiques, armor and ornaments, fossils, skeletons, mummies, and Mughal paintings); Raj Bhavan (the official residence of the governor of West Bengal, built in 1803. Following the transfer of power from the East India Company to the British Crown in 1858, it became the official residence of the viceroy of India. With the shifting of the capital to Delhi in 1911, it became the official residence of lieutenant governor of Bengal); Kolkata Town Hall (the Roman Doric-style structure was built in 1813 by the architect Maj. Gen. John Garstin, 1756–1820, with a fund of 700,000 rupees raised from a lottery to provide the Europeans with a place for social gatherings. The town hall is famous and an important landmark of Kolkata); the Calcutta High Court (the oldest high court in India. It was established as the High Court of Judicature at Fort William on July 1, 1862, under the High Courts Act, 1861. It has jurisdiction over the state of West Bengal and the Union Territory of the Andaman and Nicobar Islands. It was preceded by the Supreme Court of Judicature at Fort William); St. John's Church (originally a cathedral, it was among the first public buildings erected by the East India Company after Kolkata became the effective capital of British India); the General Post Office of the city and West Bengal; Marble Palace (it is a palatial nineteenth-century mansion in North Kolkata and one of the best preserved and most elegant houses of nineteenth-century Kolkata. The house was built in 1835 by Raja Rajendra Mullick, a wealthy

Bengali merchant with a passion for collecting works of art); the Jorasanko Thakur Bari in Jorasanko (located north of Kolkata, it is the ancestral home of the Tagore family. It is currently located on the Rabindra Bharati University campus); the University of Calcutta (a public state university established on January 24, 1857. By the foundation date, it is the first institution in South Asia to be established as a multidisciplinary and secular Western-style university); Howrah Bridge (a cantilever bridge with a suspended span over the Hooghly River. Commissioned in 1943, the bridge was originally named the New Howrah Bridge because it replaced a pontoon bridge at the same location linking the two cities of Howrah and Kolkata); and Vidyasagar Setu (also known as the Second Hooghly Bridge, is a tall bridge over the Hooghly River linking the cities of Kolkata and Howrah. With a total length of 2,700 feet, Vidyasagar Setu is the longest cable-stayed bridge in India and one of the longest in Asia).

After we crossed the Howrah Bridge, we headed back to the hotel via the magnificent Vidyasagar Setu next to the botanic garden. On the drive around the city, I was not surprised to see a McDonald's, Starbucks, Domino's Pizza, KFC, and Hard Rock Café. I also saw some horse, sheep, and cattle grazing at the roadsides.

After Sangram left me at the hotel, I had a walk to a nearby shopping area several blocks long. There were many shops there as well as roadside displays of about everything one would want, from clothes to household items. The area was very crowded with shoppers. I did find a baseball hat with India embroidered on the front. One thing I did not like was all the noise in the city, especially horn honking. The streets were packed with cars driven by rude and reckless drivers constantly honking their horns. There were also lots of buses, tuk-tuks, motorcycles, and a few bikers.

Back at the hotel, I checked my e-mail and got my boarding pass for the Vistara flight to Port Blair the next morning. Thereafter, I had dinner at the hotel restaurant and then made an early night of it after watching CNN news.

Since my flight to Port Clair was at ten, I had arranged for Sangram to pick me up at seven since I thought it would take an hour to get to the airport. However, traffic was light, and it took only thirty minutes.

At the airport, security was like the other airports I had used so far on this trip. Only passengers were allowed into the airport, and there were very thorough security checks with metal detectors and pat downs. X-ray machines checked everyone's luggage. The Calcutta airport is big and modern with a KFC.

On the two-hour flight to Port Blair, there were several people around me coughing. I had hoped I would not catch something. The plane landed in Fort Blair at noon, and an Englishman and I were the only non-Indians on the flight, so we had to fill out a long landing paper to receive visiting permits. I then went to the arrival's hall, where my driver from the Sinclairs Port Blair Hotel was waiting for me.

The hotel is only a fifteen-minute ride through the small town of Port Blair. The hotel owners claim it to be the highest structure on the island. The Blair, uniquely designed to withstand earthquakes, is the only hotel located virtually on the sea. There is a Japanese bunker and cannon nearby. I was not too impressed with the room, but it did have a nice view of the Indian Ocean.

Port Blair is located on the South Andaman Island that is surrounded by Ross, North Bay, Viper, Jolly Buoy, Redskin, Havelock, Baratang, Little Andaman, Cinque, and Neil Islands. They are in the eastern half of the Bay of Bengal and are part of India.

After I got settled in the room, I took a thirty-minute walk next to the ocean to the edge of the town. It was getting dark and had previously rained. That evening, I made an early night of it following a spicy Indian buffet dinner. After breakfast the next day, I took a three-hour tour of the town and surroundings. I visited the Cellular Jail, standing as a symbol of colonial oppression, cruelty, and untold suffering; it was here that hundreds of freedom fighters whose names are engraved on the walls of its watchtower were condemned. The prison fans out in seven wings, stands three stories high, and has a total of 698 cells. I also visited several other sites. The Anthropological Museum houses some tools and other evidences of the four Andaman Negrito tribes, namely, the Jarawas, the Sentinelese, the Great Andamanese, and the Onges, besides two Mongoloid tribes of Nicobar—the Nicobarese and the Shompens. The Cottage Industries Emporium is the storehouse of an array of artifacts of pearl, seashells, and local wood products as well as a unique collection of small Nicobari canoes, palm mats, and furniture. The Marine Museum is an exciting site in Port Blair with a huge collection of corals, shells, and about 350 species of marine life. It also includes artifacts of the tribal people, marine life, and archeology.

It was hot out, so after lunch, I stayed in the room napping, editing my pictures, getting caught up on this diary, and watching TV. Afterward, I took another walk toward town, past a statue of Pandit Jawaharlal Nehru, to a nearby boys' school, where I left about fifty ballpoint pens that I had collected over the years. It was a long walk, so I took a tuk-tuk back to the hotel.

Just after I got ready to leave the room for the airport, I opened the window partway and heard a cat crying. I looked out and saw on the ledge about five feet from the window a black cat. I was puzzled how he got there, but on check out, I told the front desk clerk about the cat, and he said that he would send someone to get it down. The cat must be related to Cochise, Lorrie's explorer cat.

On Thursday, I boarded an Air India flight to Chennai after having purchased a ticket. The airline agent told me that my original ticket had been canceled. However, following the two-hour flight, I had no trouble getting my boarding pass for Bangalore, even though it was on the same booking as the previous flight. The plane left Chennai at 1:30 p.m. From the air on takeoffs and landings, I saw that both cities are large and spread out. After the hour flight, I waited about thirty minutes in the Bangalore airport arrivals hall for a prearranged hotel pickup. Then I went outside to see if my driver was there, only to discover that the large modern Taj Hotel was near the airport, a five-minute walk.

The hotel is very modern and first class. It has three restaurants, a large lobby, conference rooms, and a swimming pool. My room was not huge but nice. The curtains drew up mechanically with a view of a large desert. The bathroom was very spacious as was the closet. One could use the closet for a bedroom. I had a cobb salad at dinner and then made an early night of it after scanning about five hundred TV channels.

I awoke at five the next morning, showered, did my exercises, and then went down for breakfast. At nine, I started an all-day tour of the city and surroundings. Rocky had his company's Mercedes. He is a big guy about fifty with a wife, sixteen-year-old daughter, and thirteen-year-old twin boys. He had worked in Saudi Arabia for several years at various jobs. He was a very personable fellow and knew the city well. He told me a lot about the city during our drive.

Bangalore, officially known as Bengaluru, is the capital of the Indian state of Karnataka since 1956. It was founded and built by Sri Kempe Gowda II (1513–1569), a noble and courageous administrator. He was a Yelahanka Feudal chieftain of the Avathi dynasty and was ruling as a feudatory of Krishnadevaraya Achyutaraya of Vijayanagara Kingdom. Today this city has gained international popularity in various fields, including information technology and biotechnology. Bengaluru has a population of about ten million and probably three times that in cars since traffic was bad in the sprawling city. However, Rocky pointed out that it was a holiday, Good Friday, and lots of people were not working.

Once in the city, we drove past Bengaluru Palace that sits in the heart of Palace Gardens. Built in 1887 by the Wodeyar dynasty, it is adorned with wood carvings and Tudor-style architecture.

We then continued past Bengaluru Fort, and Rocky told me that it was originally built in 1537 by Kempe Gowda as a mud fort, and later, it was converted into stone by Haider Ali. Located at the City Market, the fort stands testament to the struggle of the Mysore emperor against the British. Within the Bengaluru Fort lies the Tipu Sultan's Palace, which dates to the year 1790. Built entirely of teakwood, the palace was constructed as the summer residence of Tipu Sultan. The two-story palace is adorned with beautiful pillars, arches, and balconies. The fort also houses a well-preserved Ganapati Temple that was initially constructed in 1537 by Kempe.

Venkataramana Swamy Temple is located next to Tipu's summer palace. This three-hundred-year-old temple was built by Maharajah Chikka Devaraya Wodiyar. It displays some of the best features of Dravidian temple art. The ornate stone pillars, supported by splendid lion brackets, still bear the imprint of the cannonballs, which ruined portions of the temple during the third Mysore war (1790–1792). After the fall of Tipu in 1799, the Wodiyar dynasty restored the temple to its original grandeur.

As we drove past Sir Mark Cubbon Park, Rocky said that it was constructed by Lord Cubbon in 1864 over an area of three hundred acres. This ravishing garden is adorned with lush green patches, blossoming rows of flowers, and some structural buildings, all adding to its glory. Other attractions in the park are the State Central Library, Cheshire Dyer Memorial Hall, tennis court, century club, and the press club. Putani Express Train is there for children's entertainment. Another attraction is aquarium set up in a diamond-shaped complex.

Next was the Bull or Nandi Temple, one of the oldest temples of Bengaluru. It was built by Kempe Gowda in the Dravidian style. The temple has a giant fourteen-foot tall bull carved out of a single rock. The statue of Nandi is flanked at the back with statues of God Surya and Goddess Chandra on their chariots drawn by horses. The bull has a small iron plate on its head to prevent it, as tradition says, from growing.

The Sri Gavi Gangadhareshwara Temple is located at Kempe Gowda Nagar, which is sanctified because of a strange occurrence. Every year on the fourteenth or fifteenth of January—Makar Sankranti day, a ray of sunlight passes exactly through the horns of the stone bull outside the temple and illuminates the deity Shiva Linga inside the cave. This displays the amazing architectural and astronomical skills of ancient sculptors and artists.

The next site we visited was the Kempe Gowda Tower that is at Chennamma (Hudson) Circle, a sixty-foot tall tower in tribute to Bengaluru founder Kempe Gowda, and now it is another landmark of Bengaluru. Bengaluru Palace was built by Chamaraja Wodeyar in Tudor style inspired by the Windsor Castle in 1887.

We saw the ISKCON temple, located on the Hare Krishna Hill, that was built at a cost of around $10 million. There is a main temple hall that houses the altars of Lords Sri Radha Krishna—Chandra, Sri Krishna, Balarama, and Sri Nitai Gauranga. One can also see the golden chandelier that *is shaped like an inverted lotus flower. It has the world's tallest gold-plated Dwajastambha (flag post), fifty-six feet in height, and the highest gold-plated Kalash Shikara at twenty-eight feet. Rocky stated that it has already become one of the most popular and sought-after destinations in this region. The other two temples, Lord Srinivasa (Venkateswara) Temple and Lord Anjaneya Temple at Mahalakshmi Layout, are nearby.*

The Attara Kacheri (Karnataka High Court) is located just opposite to Vidhana Soudha. The high court of the state of Karnataka was established in 1884 and was known as the Mysore High Court until 1973, when the name of the state was changed.

Venkatappa Art Gallery is near Cubbon Park, a place of delight for art lovers, having about six hundred paintings.

Visvesvaraya Industrial and Technological Museum is a tribute to the brilliance of M. Visvesvaraya, one of the architects of modern Karnataka. It also houses an airplane and a steam engine.

The Gandhi Smarak Nidhi, which is housed in the Gandhi Bhavan, seeks to propagate the life and teaching of Gandhi. The Gandhi Smarak Nidhi has organized a comprehensive picture gallery depicting Gandhi's life in pictures from early childhood to the last day. Photostat copies of letters written by him to various personalities of his days can also be seen.

The Kanyaka Parameshwari Temple (Kumara Park) has a fascinating feature—Marble Mandira highlighting murals of holy places and Darpana Mandira (Mirror Mandir) depicting Bhagavad Gita, Rishis, and Vasavi history.

Vidhana Soudha is the largest legislature cum secretariat building in the country, and it is the city's best-known landmark. The sprawling building and its surroundings occupy sixty acres. The then prime minister Pandit Jawaharial Nehru laid the foundation on July 13,

immigration and customs again, even though I was already in Malaysia. My hotel driver was waiting for me, and the ride to the hotel took twenty minutes through the city. The Pullman Hotel is very plush with twenty-three floors. Connected to the hotel is a small shopping center of two floors. Most of the shops were vacant. At a hat shop, I had a custom cap made for $10. There was also a Toys R Us and a nice Japanese restaurant, where I had an early dinner. Other notable shops in the area were two McDonald's, Pizza Hut, Starbucks, and many 7-Elevens. The next morning after a nice buffet breakfast, I met my driver/tour guide, Remo, in the lobby, along with a couple from Perth, Sue and Dean. They were here on vacation. We toured through the city before going north to the Sarawak River. The ride to the Sarawak Cultural Village took about thirty minutes through the jungle countryside. The park is near two beautiful mountains.

The living museum at the Sarawak Cultural Village portrays the state's rich cultural diversity in one single place. It is a 17.5-acre sprawling expanse on the foothill of the legendary Mount Santubong fronting the South China Sea with seven authentic ethnic houses built around a man-made lake. The lake represents the propensity of Sarawakians to site their dwellings alongside rivers or along the coastal areas. This water lifeline is replicated as a focal point for water-based activities. There were handicraft-making demonstrations by skilled craft people. Traditional games, household chores, rituals, and ceremonies were performed within and outside the ethnic houses. The young and exuberant village artists provided magnificent multicultural dance performances in the modern theater.

We spent all morning at the park, walking around a pond on a wooden walkway with various homes and buildings of different cultures. The last hour was spent at a dance and singing show that was quite spectacular. One performance was a native blowing darts at balloons. There were a lot of groups of young adults and military men in the audience. At the last singing and dancing performance, members of the audience were invited on stage to join the dancers in the dance. It reminded me of the New Year's Eve party in Havana, where the dancers also invited the audience on stage.

At the cultural performance, a beautiful blonde was sitting next to me. She was a grade school teacher from Manchester, UK, and was traveling the world all year that included Europe, South America, U.S., and Asia. After we returned to the city, Remo dropped Sue and Dean off at the hotel, and then he took me on another city tour. We stopped at Fort Margherita, State Legislative Assembly Hall, Astana, Cat Museum (there are many cat statues in the city since the white cat is their city's mascot), and Chinatown. During the tour, Remo gave an excellent narrative of the history of the country and a summary of what we saw at each stop. The city of 1.5 million has nice and friendly people. Many decades ago, the country was joined with Singapore, but Singapore left the alliance in 1950.

After my thanks to Remo at the hotel, I had an early dinner at Pizza Hut then a walkabout near the hotel. (It was much cooler than yesterday since they had a much-needed short rainstorm.) I left the hotel at six the next morning for my flight back to Denver via Jakarta and Tokyo.

III

The following Monday, John returned to his routine of driving to campus with Lara and his activities in the chemistry building. On the first morning of driving to campus, John asks Lara, "Do you have any relatives with the name Pushkin?"

"John, that is a common name in Russia. But I do have a distant cousin with that name. She married a Pushkin, and he was a very violent and crazy man, worse than Ivan. She divorced the abusive man after only being married six months. Why do you ask?"

"I was curious if you had any relatives that were related to Andrei Pushkin, Margrit's lover in Vienna, that I told you about. I had a graduate student at Clemson named Igor Medvedev. He was from Moscow. Since I know Medvedev is a common name in Russia, I am fairly certain that he is not related to your ex-husband."

As John still considers Lara is trying to kill him, he does not do any weekend traveling with her and continues to stay at home most days. Bob has agreed to his working at home as long as he continues to communicate with his students about their research.

A week before the conference in San Diego, Lara asks John if he would like to hike the trail next to Pine Shadows with her since she has not been on the trail before. He agrees and says, "We have had a very mild winter so far with little snow. Today it is almost like spring, maybe because of climate change. However, the trail may be covered in snow in a few places. Since the county placed wood chips on the trail last year, we do not have to worry about mud."

During their walk on the narrow trail, Lara is behind John. At a turn in the trail, Johns sees a bear ahead. He frantically tells Lara to run back to the garage. John closely follows her, but the bear catches up to him and knocks him down. As John is fighting off the bear, Lara runs back to help him. On the way, she pulls an aerosol can of pepper spray out of her backpack that she had recently purchased. When she reaches John and the bear, she sprays lots of pepper in the bear's face. This causes the bear to let go of John. Then the bear runs up the hill and disappears. Lara kneels and asks John, "Are you okay? I see blood running down your arms."

"No, I am hurting."

She helps him take off his coat and shirt. "There are several deep puncture wounds on your upper arms and shoulders." Lara then rips John's shirt into strips. "I will try and stop the bleeding with these pieces of your shirt."

After she gets most of the bleeding stopped, she helps John return to her apartment, where she washes John's wounds and properly bandages him. She tells John that he needs to go to the hospital to get some of his wounds stitched.

As Lara is driving John to the hospital, he thinks how wrong he has been about Lara wanting to kill him. *If she wanted me dead, she would not have rescued me from the bear attack.* He then tells Lara how grateful he is for her saving his life and comments, "I was lucky you had some pepper spray with you. How did you find out about its use against bear attacks?"

"Gail told me about a bear she saw near the house last year and advised me that it would be wise to buy some pepper spray. She said that I could also use it against an evil man attacking me."

"It is unusual to see a bear so early in the year, but the snow is almost gone, and the young bear must have been very hungry after hibernation all winter."

After getting treated by the emergency room doctor, they return to Pine Shadows. John then tells Lara that he will go to bed and get some rest. Before they separate, John takes Lara in his arms and thanks her again for saving his life.

"John, I would go to the end of the earth to save your life. I love you and never want anything or anyone to hurt you."

After a loving hug, John says, "Thank you, but now I will spend the rest of the weekend in bed. I will see you on Monday morning for our ride to school."

As John is resting in bed, he thinks more about how wrong he has been about Lara trying to kill him. *If she wanted me dead, she would only have had to keep running away from me and the bear. The arsenic-laced vodka was most likely sent by her ex-husband since Lara told me that he had tried to kill her after she divorced him.*

Upon reaching the chemistry building on Monday, they invite their students to come to their office and give them a review of the posters that they will present at the meeting next week. John tells the students that he and Lara will ask them some questions that they will probably be asked by the conference attendees who view their posters. He also tells them that he has arranged their travel and hotel accommodations. "Lara and Susan will share a twin-bed room as will Larry and Mark. Since I snore, I will have a one-bed room. You all will fly directly to San Diego on Sunday morning, and Lara and I will go in my jeep so I can show her some of the Southwestern U.S."

After the students leave their office, John tells Lara about their travel plans. "We will leave Nederland early tomorrow morning and spend the first night in Santa Fe, New Mexico, and the second night in Albuquerque so we can have dinner with a high school friend of mine and his wife. Thursday morning, I would like you to meet a couple I worked with at Clemson over breakfast. That night, we will get a hotel in Farmington, Arizona, and visit the Grand Canyon. The following morning, we will drive to Kingman and stay there overnight. On Saturday afternoon, we should reach San Diego. Following getting checked into the hotel, we can have a walk around the center of the city. After a late Sunday breakfast, we will need to go to the airport and pick up our students. After their checking in and unpacking at the hotel, we can all go for lunch, followed by attending the opening ceremony of the meeting in the hotel's conference center. Sometime during the meeting, I need to find a doctor who can remove the stiches in my shoulders and back.

"I had hoped to see my younger brother, Gregory Erickson, and his family following the meeting. They live in Simi Valley, a city north of Los Angeles. They will still be on a trip to Japan, Australia, and New Zealand. Greg e-mailed me a note about their travels so far on the trip when they visited Japan. You can take the e-mail to read tonight if you wish."

Dear John James,

I am sorry I will miss you on your visit to California, but we are now traveling to Australia. Our first stop was Japan. The following are a few words, ha, about our traveling in Japan that I think you will enjoy reading.

Following a Saturday breakfast at nine, we piled into our Honda and went to LAX in light traffic. After parking the car near terminal 4, we checked two bags and got our boarding passes. Then we went through security to our boarding gate for our noon American Airline flight to Tokyo. We arrived at Narita airport at four in the afternoon the next day. After immigration, customs, and exchanging money (11,000 yen for $100), we got our reserved shuttle for a ride to the nice Gracery Shinjuku hotel, where we stayed for four nights. The hotel is in the heart of the city surrounded by many shops and restaurants. Ann and I had a great spacious room on the seventieth floor overlooking part of Tokyo. Tom and Mark had the room directly above us.

After a good night's sleep and breakfast, the four of us went on a walk near the hotel. After lunch and a nap, we walked farther from the hotel to visit some shrines and temples. That evening after dinner, we took a walk around the area of the hotel with many shops lit up with colorful lights. We had a treat watching the large stone dragon Godzilla outside the eighth floor of the hotel. Godzilla shot out fire and smoke—very realistic.

On Tuesday, I had arranged for a tour to Mount Fuji. Our van driver/guide (Kat, who has seven cats at home) picked us up after breakfast for a two-hour drive to the mountain. The van could only drive about halfway up Mount Fuji (Step Four, about 6,100 feet) since the road was blocked because of snow. The mountain was not as breathtaking as it is from a distance. We had about an hour's visit. Then we had lunch at a nearby hotel with an amusement park next door and a great view of Mount Fuji.

Kat then took us to Fuji Hakone Izu National Park, where we took a short ferry ride across a lake to a cable car that went to the top of a small mountain with a temple on top. There, we had a view of Mount Fuji through the clouds. We returned to our hotel in the late afternoon for dinner and another walk around the hotel area.

On Wednesday, we took a hop-on, hop-off bus tour of Tokyo. We first went to the Imperial Palace, where we got off the bus and had a walk around part of the large palace. We then returned to the bus stop and took the next bus to Tokyo tower. We had a great view of the entire city on the tower and took lots of pictures. Afterward, we got on another hop-on, hop-off bus and went by the train station, several temples, and shrines. The World Heritage sites such as the Rengeo-in temple, with its 1,001 statues of the Buddhist deity, and Meiji Jingu (a Shinto shrine), with its beautiful garden and forest, were the most impressive.

The next day, we took the Nozomi bullet train to Kyoto, leaving at ten in the morning and arriving at one. On the train ride, we went past Mount Fuji. I read the Japan News *on the way and was shocked to read about the civil war taking place in Libya. At least four people were killed in heavy shelling in Tripoli. Eastern forces commanded by Khalifa Haftar were trying to seize the city. Nearly two weeks into its assault, the veteran general's eastern-based Libyan National Army struck in the city's southern outskirts battling armed groups loyal to the internationally recognized Tripoli government. I am sure you are concerned about the safety of your God family living in Tripoli.*

In Kyoto, we spent three nights at the Kyoto Tower Hotel. The first-class hotel is across from the train station and in a nice area of shops and restaurants, including Starbucks and McDonald's. Kyoto, once the capital of Japan, is a city on the island of Honshu. It is famous for numerous classical Buddhist temples, Shinto shrines, and other historical priceless structures.

After check-in at the hotel and lunch at McDonald's, we went up to the top of the hotel, the 430-foot-high Kyoto Tower. There, we had a 360-degree view of the city: the Nishi Hongwanji, Ninnaji, Higashi Hongan-ji, Chion-in, Kiyomizu-dera, Tofukuji and Toji temples as well as the Nijo and Fushimi-Momoyama castles, and the Tadasu-no-Mori, Heian Jingu, and Fushimi Inari Taisha shrines. Kyoto University, railroad museum, and aquarium were also visible. The hotel has a sky lounge, terrace restaurant, beer garden, and public bathhouse.

The next day, our group of four took a taxi to the Arashiyama and Tenryu-ji Temple that is near a bamboo forest. Afterward, we either visited or slowly drove by other temples and shrines in the city. One impressive shrine was Higashi Honganji Temple with the Founder's Hall, claimed to be the largest wooden structure in the world. Around noon, we had lunch near the Arashiyama Temple and later a walk around the temple grounds and bamboo forest. Our last stop was at the Rokuon-ji Temple Precincts, including the Golden Pavilion. Later, we went back to the hotel and had dinner.

On our last day in Japan, we took a shuttle to the Kansai (Kyoto) airport (on an elevated highway), where we caught our flight to Sydney. It had been a great start to our trip.

Chapter 3
Travels in North America

I

John and Lara depart Nederland the next morning before the sun starts to come up so John can avoid sun in his eyes on the ride on HY-36 to Denver. A little after they start going south on I-25, there is a beautiful sunrise. Before they reach Colorado Springs, John points out to Lara the Air Force Academy next to the mountains. John suggests they drive through the Garden of the Gods to Manitou Springs and take the cog rail train to the top of Pikes Peak. John remarks, "Because of our mild winter, the train had just started operation a week ago. The drive through Manitou Springs, known for its mineral springs, is nice since the beautiful old buildings are much like the ones in Central City. After we reach the summit of Pikes Peak, that has the highest paved road in the U.S., we can have coffee and donuts. We need to eat the special donuts there because I was told if we take them with us, they will collapse at the lower altitude. There is an annual car race and marathon up the mountain. The peak is 14,114 feet above sea level and is one of Colorado's fifty-three mountains above 14,000 feet."

After the train ride and going through Manitou Springs and Colorado Springs, Lara says, "The train ride was great, and what a view from the top of Pike's Peak. I was surprised to see that the red slanted mountains at the Garden of the Gods are just like the Flatirons in Boulder, so beautiful and breathtaking."

"There are similar groups of mountains in Denver's Red Rocks Park near Morrison and at Roxbury Park south of Denver.

A good friend of mine lives in a subdivision next to Roxbury Park. I should take you there sometime."

About an hour later, they get off I-25 and have a short stop in Pueblo. Over lunch Johns tells Lara a little of what he knows of the city, including that their main industry is steelmaking.

After the couple's visit to Pueblo, they get back on I-25 and have a brief stop in Walsenburg, a small Western town, and then proceed to Trinidad, a good-size city with some picturesque mountains nearby. They have a short walk around the downtown area, and Lara notes that the most interesting thing about Trinidad is the red bricks laid in some of the downtown streets instead of concrete or asphalt. They both like the architecture of some of the old buildings. Next, they have a brief stop in Las Vegas, New Mexico, and a walk around the old city center. The couple arrives in Santa Fe about six and check into two adjoining rooms at the nice Chimayo Hotel next to the Old Town Plaza. After getting settled in their rooms, they have a nice dinner at a packed restaurant called the Shed and then take a walk around the old town square with its beautiful buildings of Spanish Pueblo style. After breakfast the next morning, they head to Albuquerque.

Before arriving in Albuquerque, they make a detour to see the nuclear museum in Los Alamos. John explains to Lara that Los Alamos is the home of a national laboratory that was instrumental in the development and building of the first nuclear bombs. Now the Lawrence Berkeley National Laboratory near San Francisco and the Hanford site in Washington assists the Los Alamos laboratory to produce the nuclear warheads. Rocky Flats was part of the nuclear weapon production complex before it was closed. John had spent some time in Berkeley when he worked at Rocky Flats, assisting them in the development of the neutron bomb.

Following their short visit to the museum, they go to the Kasha-Katuwe Tent Rocks National Monument. The road near the monument is like a roller-coaster ride as they have to slowly go over many dips in the road where water flows during rainstorms.

The mountains in the area are white with many smaller peaks that look like upside-down ice cream cones. John explains to Lara that the cone-shaped tent rock formations are the products of volcanic eruptions that occurred six to seven million years ago and left pumice, ash, and tuff deposits over a thousand-feet thick. Precariously perched on many of the tapering hoodoos are boulder caps that protect the softer pumice and tuff below.

In Albuquerque, they stay at the Holiday Inn Express. That night, they meet with John's high school friend and his wife at Applebee's next to the hotel for dinner. The men talk about their last time together, boyhood antics, jobs, and what they are doing now. Bill still donates his mornings to helping his church and, in the afternoon, writes on various topics.

The next morning, they have an early breakfast at the hotel with one of John's former students and his former postdoc. The two got married after leaving Clemson. They talk about Brian making homemade beer with a colleague at work, Brian's job, and what Shanna is doing at the University of New Mexico now. Before leaving Albuquerque after breakfast, John and Lara have a brief visit to the Old Town Square, where the oldest church in Albuquerque, San Felipe de Neri, is located. Old Town is right next to the famous Route 66 highway.

After their visit to Albuquerque, they resume their drive west on HY-40. One of the funny things they see is a recreational vehicle pulling a small airplane with its wings detached. Most of all the other RVs they pass are pulling cars. They get off HY-40 at Thoreau, New Mexico, and head north on HY-371 to Farmington. After reaching Farmington, they go east a short way on HY-64 to HY-550 and then to HY-57 to visit the Chaco Culture National Historic Park that is now a World Heritage Site. They walk down to Pueblo Bonito, the core of the Chaco complex and the largest great house. It was built by Chacoans in stages between the mid-800s and early 1100s and is four stories high with over six hundred rooms. They also go to Chetro Ketl, another of the largest great houses, which has an immense elevated earthen plaza. Later, the couple returns to Farmington and check into the Red Lion Inn. They have a late dinner at the Olive Garden across town since John is craving some tortellini.

Following an early breakfast the next morning, they travel to the nearby Aztec Ruins. The Aztec structures were built in the late 1000s to the late 1200s by the ancestral Pueblo people who lived there centuries before the Aztec Empire prospered. The settlement included large public buildings, smaller structures, earthworks, and ceremonial buildings. After the short visit, John and Lara get back on HY-64 and stop at Four Corners, where Colorado, New Mexico, Arizona, and Utah meet. There is a marker at the place where the four states meet. Lara gets her picture taken by John, where she has her knees in New Mexico and Colorado and hands in Utah and Arizona. Both laugh a lot during the picture taking.

They then get on HY-160 to HY-64, heading toward the southeast rim of the Grand Canyon. Before they arrive at the Grand Canyon, they stop for a quick look at the Canyon of the Little Colorado River. The Little Colorado Gorge, comprising 379,000 acres, was established as a Navajo Tribal Park in 1962. The park lies in the extreme western portion of the Navajo Nation adjacent to the eastern boundary of Grand Canyon National Park. The park straddles the Canyon of the Little Colorado River at its confluence with the Colorado River. Although not nearly as wide as the Grand Canyon, the deep, precipitous cliffs of the gorge are colorful and spectacular. The park affords an excellent westward view of the Grand Canyon itself, revealing some of the most completed geological sequences ever to be found in the world.

Next, they go to the beautiful and spectacular Grand Canyon. John tells Lara a little about the canyon. "The story of the Grand Canyon stretches back almost two billion years. Evidence of every geological period from the Precambrian to the end of the Mesozoic can be observed."

The three students take turns expressing their favorable views of the meeting. Later, they enjoy the dessert.

John then asks the students to tell everyone about the places they have visited in the past. Susan says, "Since I grew up in Washington, I got to visit a lot of the Northwestern U.S. numerous times and even took a vacation to Vancouver, Canada, with my parents. When I was about fourteen, we had a good time at Disneyland."

Larry remarks, "I was in California one time as well as all the states in the Southeast and made a couple of trips to D.C. and New York. I grew up in Miami."

Mark explains, "I have seen all the major Australian cities growing up in Perth and even made a trip to New Zealand when I was going to the University of Melbourne. This is my first visit to the U.S., and after getting my PhD, I plan to see more of your country."

Before they return to the hotel, John tells them a little about living in Simi Valley. "After living and working in Australia for three years, Margrit, my first wife, and I returned to the U.S. and lived on the west end of Simi Valley, across from the Reagan Library. My job was at the Rocketdyne site in the Santa Susana Mountains at the east end of Simi Valley. After I arrived at the site on the first day of work in the nuclear part of the site, the ground started to shake extremely hard. Of course, I thought it was a major earthquake and jumped under my desk. My boss had seen my actions, laughed, and told me the other side of the site is where rocket engines are tested. He said when the rocket engine blasts, the whole site shakes. I worked on several different research projects during my three years with Rocketdyne. Unfortunately, there was a 6.8 earthquake during my last night in California. The shaking scared me so much I had a hard time getting out of bed and taking shelter in the bathroom. However, the movers had an easy time the next day packing my pictures since everything on the walls was lying on the floor. Please do not worry about an earthquake since I think they are rare in San

Diego. But if the ground starts to shake, seek shelter away from windows immediately."

Following their return to the hotel, they sit in the lobby for a while, where John tells the group about one of his trips to Mexico. "I took six of my Clemson students for a short trip to Juarez following the Environmental Design Contest at New Mexico State University in Las Cruces. They had participated in the contest and won first place for their project on treatment of wastewater. We took a walk around the old part of Juarez, had lunch, and did some shopping. I have a great picture of the group wearing Mexican sombreros. I am sorry we do not have time to make a short visit to Tijuana. Anyway, I think Professor Medvedev would need a Mexican visa to get into the country."

The next day, the group attends the meeting all day, followed by dinner in the hotel. Everyone enjoys the tour of San Diego on Wednesday, and after the talks on Thursday, they all have a good time at the conference banquet. The group of five do not attend the last day of the meeting but travel to Anaheim for a day at Disneyland. At dinner that night, the group mainly talks about the good time they had at Disneyland. Lara says, "The Pirates of the Caribbean was my favorite ride, but I was a bit scared at the beginning of the boat ride when we went down that waterfall."

John remarks, "I also liked that ride, and it was fun to take it twice. The Big Thunder Mountain Railroad was also quite exciting."

The three students all agree that they liked the Splash Mountain ride the best since they think it is the most exciting one of the day.

After an early breakfast the next morning, the group checks out of the hotel and goes to the airport. After their arrival at the airport, the students give their thanks and goodbyes to John and Lara and walk to the departure hall. John and Lara then travel to Universal City. They have a long walk around Universal Studios and ride the studio tour train. As the train passes the Bates Motel, Lara is startled when the actor playing the crazy

Norman Bates chases the tour cars swinging a big hunting knife. The man-eating shark, Jaws, coming out of Jaws Lake also scares Lara.

After finishing the studio tour, taking a ride on the Flight of the Hippogriff, and going through Jurassic World, they leave the park and have a late lunch at a nice restaurant overlooking the ocean. Then they go to the Getty Museum for a short visit, followed by driving up the coast, through Malibu, to Simi Valley to visit the Reagan Library. John tells Lara that he is impressed by the large piece of the Berlin Wall that is displayed behind the museum. Lara comments that the view of Simi Valley from the library is terrific. They end the day at the Holiday Inn in Downtown Los Angeles.

After breakfast on Sunday morning and a short walk near the hotel, John and Lara check out of the hotel and head for Las Vegas, a five-hour drive. On the drive, Lara says, "I sure enjoyed our visits to Disneyland and Universal City. I am looking forward to winning at the slots in Vegas."

In Las Vegas, they stay at the MGM Grand, where the Miss America contest is being held. The couple gets to meet Miss Colorado and has their picture taken with her. That evening, they have dinner with John's cousin and his Columbian-born wife. After dinner and arriving back at the hotel, John coaches Lara playing five-card draw, and she wins $30. Then John plays and loses $25.

The next day, they have an early breakfast with a West High friend of John's. Following the meal, they head to Eastern Utah going Northeast on I-15 and east on I-70 to Arches National Park. Surprisingly, there are not a lot of tourists there. The couple agrees that the park is spectacular. John tells Lara later that Arches now moves Grand Canyon National Park to fourth place on his list of favorite national parks.

About eight in the evening, they reach Grand Junction. Before dinner at an Italian restaurant, they have a short walk in the old downtown area that has lots of souvenir shops, restaurants, and a few street entertainers. They spend their last night on the trip at the Knights Inn.

After an early breakfast the next morning, they take a twenty-mile ride through the beautiful Colorado National Monument. This is John's first time through the fascinating red rocks that had been weathered into beautiful sculptures. They continue the trip with short visits to Grand Mesa, Glenwood Springs, Aspen, and Vail. On the final leg of their drive to Nederland, Lara reads about one of John's trips to Canada.

The day following my arrival in Saskatoon, a small group of us took the one-hour flight from Saskatoon to the McArthur River Mine for an underground tour; the mine has one of the largest and richest uranium deposits in the world. For the tour, I was loaded down with hard hat, protective clothing, supplied air, and boots that made walking around the mine a lot of effort. Our group toured two different levels, six hundred and eight hundred feet below the surface, and saw all the cooled brine pipes used to freeze the incoming water. The airflow through the mine was high to keep toxic radon levels down.

After lunch, our group was bused back to the airport for a fifteen-minute flight to the Key Lake Uranium Processing Mill, one of the largest uranium mills in the world. After arrival, we spotted a big brown bear by the road. Following the mill tour, we returned to the city by air and missed the uranium conference welcome reception. I checked into the Sheridan Hotel.

The conference lasted three days. There was plenty to eat at the breakfasts and breaks every day, and the wonderful lunches were at the Sheridan Hotel across the street from the conference center. On Monday night, a couple of friends and I had dinner under the stars behind the Delta Bessborough Hotel in the garden near the Saskatchewan River. I met a lot of nice folks that night and during the meeting. On Tuesday night, the conference banquet was at the Sheridan. A discussion session was held on the last day of the meeting.

On Thursday morning, I caught an hour-long flight to Edmonton and picked up a rental car, a black Ford Fusion, which I liked very much. I drove down HY-2 to Calgary and then caught HY-1 to Banff. I arrived in Banff National Park in the afternoon and checked into the Inns of Banff, along with a lot of Asian guests. (The hotel had a Japanese steakhouse.) My room had a balcony with a grand view of the mountains to the west and north. I then drove around town, followed by a good walk that included admiring a beautiful flower garden at Park Headquarters that overlooks the downtown area.

On Friday, I headed out early in the dark down HY-1 to Lake Louise, over to British Columbia, and through Yoho National Park to Glacier and Mount Revelstoke National Parks. I stopped a few times and took pictures, but most of the mountains were obscure from all the forest fires raging in British Columbia. I turned around and stopped in Golden for breakfast then headed south down HY-95 to Radium Hot Springs. There, I caught HY-93 through Kootenay National Park and back to Banff for the evening. My drives through the parks showed me the beauty of Canada.

The next day, I went north on HY-93 to Jasper National Park. Again, the scenery was super, and the mountains were majestic, especially near the snowfield's area. I arrived in Jasper after about four hours of driving, followed by touring part of the park.

Then I took HY-16 to Edmonton. I drove around the large metropolis instead of going through it to avoid the traffic. I continued from the city on Yellowhead Highway to Elk Island National Park, about an hour's drive east of Edmonton. I saw a lot of lakes and buffalo but no elk. After enjoying the view, I headed to the airport to catch a 6:30 p.m. flight to Saskatoon. After landing, I got a rental car and checked into the Hilton Garden Inn downtown.

Early the next morning, I drove north to Prince Albert, had some breakfast at McDonald's, and then drove another forty-five minutes to Prince Albert National Park. There were a few Indian communities just before I entered the south entrance and drove about two-thirds through the park before I saw a few people and cars. What I first saw were flashing red lights on an ambulance and police car and then a small white car that was overturned in the ditch. I continued driving but a little slower up to Waskesiu Lake and the residential area. After a short drive around some expensive homes, I drove back to the city to catch my 2:30 p.m. flight back to Denver.

I had some nice company on the flight. Brittinea and I visited the whole trip. She is a waitress at the Ramada Inn in Prince Albert and a part-time model and was on her way to Phoenix to relax with friends for a week. Brittinea was regretting going through immigration in Denver since they always gave her a bad time and asked her a lot of questions. I said, "It is probably because of the Al-Qaeda symbol that you have tattooed on your middle finger." She looked at her fingers, each having a tattoo near the nail. She was a beautiful blond, and next I said, "Just kidding. It is probably because they liked talking with you."

"John, I wish I could see some of Canada, but just like Mexico, I think I would need a visa."

"I wanted to surprise you, but I was considering arranging for us to take a cruise on Glacier Bay, in Western Alaska, after the spring semester ends. There, you would see similar scenery as in the western part of Canada. I think the diary you have been reading has a story about one of my trips to the most northerly part of Alaska. It shows how my guardian angels look out for me."

I went to Alaska on May 31 and returned to Denver on June 3. My first glimpse of Alaska from the plane was a beautiful mountain range near Fairbanks. It was still light outside around eleven. My cab driver from the airport did not know why the town was called Fairbanks. I told him the "Why is a river so rich" joke. I stayed overnight at the Travelodge near the airport.

At eight the next morning, I flew to Barrow via Prudhoe Bay. The weather at Barrow was cloudy, and the area was flat. There were houses next to the runway, and snow was piled high all over. It was a small airport, the size of a small house. Security for outbound passengers was in the same room as inbound passengers.

As usual, I had nothing arranged at Barrow for a tour. It was cold, and I was very thankful that I brought my heavy coat. As I stepped out of the small airport, with no taxis in sight, along came a tour van down the road. I waved for the driver to stop. I was lucky as the young lady driving the empty van gave me a lift to the hotel and asked me to join her tour of the area in the afternoon. After check-in at the small hotel, I had an early lunch at a Mexican restaurant next to the hotel while waiting for my tour to start at noon.

On the tour, I found out that all the roads in town are dirt, and everything is dirty, including my shoes. This is the most northern part of the North American continent, and the town reminded me of Greenland. The tour was not too interesting, but the driver's narration made the trip worthwhile.

On Sunday, I headed for Nome via Kotzebue. Most of the Alaska Airlines planes are good except the one I was on. The first half of the plane was for cargo. It was raining when I left Barrow, but Nome was nice. The plane had a rough landing in Nome because of a short runway. It was the first time I had ever got propelled from my seat toward the front of the plane. At the end of my stay in Nome, the plane had a short takeoff and left the ground just as the runway ended. It had been the same in Barrow.

Nome has a population of around 3,500, and the Snake River runs through the town. The town boomed in 1898 after the discovery of gold. Again, I was fortunate as I asked one of the Alaska Airlines clerks about a tour of the town, she said she knew of one and called Richard, who came over in ten minutes in a blue van, the only taxi in town. Richard dropped me at the hotel's Polar Café, where I ordered eggs and reindeer sausage while Richard went home to take care of his two dogs. The café was nice, and it looks out over the Bering Sea, where one could see Sledge Island and the Norton Sound. After breakfast and check-in, Richard came and took me on an all-day tour for $12.

Richard is quite a guy and a former Coloradoan. He had spent two years at Aurora High. After high school, he was a singer/dancer in New York until the booze got him. His passion was dancing and singing, but after New York, he traveled all over—Denver; Salina, Kansas; Japan; San Antonio, Texas—and ended up in Nome.

We ended the tour in some tundra on Anvil Mountain overlooking the Bearing Sea and Nome. Richard told me that the abandoned home nearby was Watt Earp's home during the gold-digging days. Western gunfighter Earp also had a home in town.

Before I left for Fairbanks the next day, Richard took me to see two dredging systems, one by the airport. Airport security was almost absent and worse than in Barrow. Before security, I spoke with the young gal working for Alaska Airlines. She told me that she was from Denver and had attended East High. She had been in Nome for two years.

Perhaps because of my kind talk with the gal, I got upgraded to first class in going to Anchorage. On the almost two-hour flight, I saw Mt. McKinley out the window.

"John, it is amazing that you have such good luck on your travels. By the way, what is the answer to your question 'Why is a river so rich?'"

"It is because a river has two banks."

Lara laughs.

"Another question for you. Do you know how to spell Mississippi with only one eye?"

"I have heard that before," she says as she covers her left eye and recites each letter of Mississippi.

This time they both laugh.

II

After their return to Nederland, John and Lara continue their usual work activities, mainly working in the laboratory with their students. They also attend faculty meetings on Mondays and seminars on Fridays. After work, John sometimes takes Lara on a drive to Chautauqua Park for walks up to the Flatirons, dinner at the park's Dining Hall, and meals at the Pearl Street Mall, the Sink on "The Hill," the Dark Horse, and other restaurants in Boulder as well as his favorites in Nederland.

Of course, they have several dinner parties with John's children, Randy, Gail, and the Cochins and Stevens. They also take weekend trips around to some of the places in the Colorado mountains that Lara has not seen. At least once a week, Lara continues to read John's diaries. One entry is about a trip to the Caribbean.

> *On Friday, I went to DIA for my flight to Charlotte. While at my gate, Homeland Security was training a new bomb-sniffing dog. The dog came to me and started licking my shoe; apparently, he smelled a residue of Randy and Gail's puppy on my shoe.*

The plane left Denver at one in the morning and arrived in Charlotte at six. I then had a four-hour layover in Charlotte before flying to St. Maarten. St. Maarten is the Dutch side of the island and is shared with St. Martin, which is administered by the French government.

The French West Indies consists of the islands of Martinique, Guadeloupe, St. Martin, and St. Barthelemy. These islands are well developed, and French is the official language. However, English is widely spoken in St. Martin and St. Barthelemy but much less so in Martinique and Guadeloupe. U.S. currency is accepted in St. Martin and St. Barthelemy. The Netherlands Antilles florin is the official currency. The U.S. dollar is also widely accepted in St. Maarten.

In St. Maarten, I stayed at the Caravanserai Beach Hotel next to the airport. The runway is one lane and used for both taking off and landing. The hotel has separate buildings, out front is a casino, as well as Chinese, Thai, French, and American restaurants. I had a late lunch at the Thai restaurant and breakfast Saturday morning at the hotel. I took a taxi across the island to Philipsburg. Then I went by water taxi from the Philipsburg pier area to town, a ten-minute ride. I had a walk around town and then went back to the pier for the boarding of the ship.

The Star Clipper, *a large sailing ship, had about one hundred passengers from eleven countries aboard. My cabin has a double bed, bathroom, closet, and TV. The bed is very high from the floor, but there is a short stepladder for my use.*

After boarding, the passengers had a drill with life vests on, then dinner at 7:30 p.m. I sat with three German ladies; one was a radiation (X-ray) doctor, Klara; Klara's daughter Kira; and Petra. All were from Hanover.

On ship at other dinners, I would sit with a different group of fellow passengers. Usually, a couple from the night before had sat with a couple that knew me. One lady would say, "I understand that you are a professor." I would say, "No, I am a writer." Then the next night, the same thing would happen except another lady would say, "I understand that you are a writer." I would say, "No, I am a scientist." This would go on and on, one night an architect, and the other nights, I was an actor, a teacher, and a carpenter. I had a good time stretching the truth, even though I had designed and helped build a house.

The first night, the Star Clipper *left Wathey Pier at ten for Anguilla. Anguilla is a British overseas territory in the Eastern Caribbean, part of the British West Indies. It is a small but rapidly developing island with particularly well-developed tourist facilities. After sailing overnight, we arrived in Anguilla on Sunday. We landed at Sandy Ground but did not visit the valley. The usual daily routine was to have gymnastics 8:00–8:30 a.m., breakfast 8:00–10:00 a.m., lunch 11:30 a.m.–1:30 p.m., cocktail hour 5:00–6:00 p.m., dinner 7:30–10:00 p.m., and a midnight snack 10:45 p.m.– 1:00 a.m. No one on ship went hungry. The first morning, all the passengers had a welcome talk from the captain and in the afternoon visited the island for water sports. We were transported from the ship to the pier by speedboats, called tenders, holding around twenty people. In the evening, there was piano music in the lounge area with dancing.*

There was a masseuse on board, and Bernadette was from the Philippines. I got a good massage from her before our arrival at Virgin Gorda in the British Virgin Islands (BVI). BVI is an overseas territory, part of the British West Indies, lying about sixty miles east of Puerto Rico. There are about fifty islands in the BVI, many of which are uninhabited. Tortola is the main island, and the other islands include Virgin Gorda, Jost Van Dyke, and Anegada. Tourist facilities are widely available.

On Tuesday, we started sailing after breakfast and had a short journey to Norman Island, where I joked that one should be careful there after landing since Norman Bates is rumored to be living on the island. Norman Island is next to St. John, U.S. Virgin Island. We went over after lunch by tender and found that there was not much on the small beach except a bar/restaurant and gift shop. However, it was a great place for marine sport activities: snorkeling, kayaking, sailing, waterskiing, surfing, paddle boating, and swimming. I went ashore for about an hour, where I had a good view of two storks having fun diving into the sea.

After I got back to ship, Bernadette gave me an hour massage on the top deck overlooking the Caribbean Sea. The unusual massage room consists of canvases on three sides and the roof. The only other interesting massage places I have had in the past were poolside in Bali and poolside in Mozambique next to the Indian Ocean. Then there was the massage in the doctor's office aboard the Akademic Abraham *near Antarctica. I could write a book on massage adventures around the world.*

On Virgin Gorda, there is what is called the Baths, which are a series of small sea pools lying beneath a canopy of giant granite boulders. These sheltered light-filled grottoes create a unique setting in which to swim and explore. Open-air safari buses brought us to the entrance of the Baths. A path goes down to a beautiful sandy beach, where we had plenty of time to swim or snorkel in the emerald clear waters or just relax in the warm Caribbean sun. A trail leads through the boulders to another equally beautiful beach at Devil's Bay. Some of the group swam and basked in the sun awhile. After our return to the car park and waiting for the bus, we were served a complimentary refreshing fruit or rum punch. On the way back to port, several stops were made for photo taking. The tour bus traveled the twisting road to the crest of the mountain from where our ship revealed in Gorda Sound. After we went back to the dock, we boarded our tender boat to Sand Box and had a barbecue. The afternoon was spent on the beach. The tender ride back stopped at the Bitter End Sailing Club. Following our return to ship, I had a little nap before dinner.

From the Virgin Gorda on our way to Tortola Island, we passed through the Sir Francis Drake Channel, where many smaller islands are located with many expensive homes. The ship anchored overnight near Tortola, and we planned to visit Jost Van Dyke in the morning.

I did not want to go ashore at Soper's Sole, Tortola, because of the rainstorm under way that would cause a wet and rough landing from a tender. On Wednesday, I did go ashore for a couple of hours at Jost Van Dyke, BVI. The island has a small beach with a couple of bars and gift shops. After I returned to ship, I had lunch and did some writing.

Our next visit was to St. Kitts and Nevis, a developing Eastern Caribbean nation consisting of two islands. Tourist facilities were widely available. We took a three-and-a-half-hour bus ride to see half of St. Kitts. We started in Basseterre and went west, stopping at Fairview Great House and Botanical Gardens. Also at St. Kitts are Romney Gardens and Caribelle Batik Studios. This ten-acre garden setting is quite simply stunning. This glorious location is where local artists produce the fabric for their work. Our final stop was at Brimstone Hill Fortress National Park to enjoy the spectacular panoramic views of the coastline, countryside, and five neighboring islands. The old fortress, perched on a forty-acre hilltop, 780 feet above sea level, is where more battles were fought than at any other single site in British and French naval history. The first cannons were mounted on Brimstone Hill in 1690 as the English and French fought for control of the island. The next two hundred years saw the intermittent construction of an amazing work of architectural and engineering genius. This magnificent structure is the second largest of its type in the entire western hemisphere and one of the best preserved.

We returned to Basseterre and caught our ship at a different place—South Friar's Bay. In the evening, the ship headed to Gustavia, St. Barts, and after rough seas, we anchored at St. Barts (St. Barthelemy) around nine on Friday morning. We went ashore after breakfast. The tender was rocking back and forth in the rough sea in the bay, both going and coming. Gustavia is small and full of tourist shops. I was with a small group of fellow passengers who stayed awhile on top of a hill overlooking the small village and bay.

On Saturday morning, we arrived back at Philipsburg, St. Maarten, and disembarked from the Star Clipper. *Later, I took a taxi ride around Marigot, St. Martin, then went back to St. Maarten and caught a US Airways plane from Philipsburg to Denver via Charlotte.*

III

At the end of the spring semester, the three students return to their homes for several weeks of vacation. John discusses his plans for the summer. "Lara, I plan to attend a solvent extraction conference in Sweden at the end of next month, mainly to see old friends and take some tours. I will not give a paper at the conference. Would you like to join me?"

"Of course, John. Maybe we could go to Moscow after the meeting so you can meet my folks and brother."

"Well, I will have to be careful since Andrei's brother is still somewhere in Russia and would like me dead. But it will be nice to meet your parents and brother and have reunions with a few of my dear friends in Moscow."

"Of course, John. We can keep the information about our visit just between us and my relatives and your friends so you will not have any concerns about Andrei's brother."

"Before we leave for Europe, though, I would also like to take you to my favorite national park, Yellowstone, for several days. However, I would like to drive Red there instead of flying to Jackson. It will be a long car trip. How does that sound?"

"Great. I do love your car trips since I can see more of the countryside and towns we drive through unlike flying. How about we leave this Thursday since I need a couple of days to finish drafting the journal article on our research for you to edit?"

"Okay. I have another question. I have registered for a National Geographic expedition to see some of the sites in Western Alaska. You are welcome to join me if you do not mind sharing a cabin with me. The cruise leaves from Juneau."

"That would be wonderful, John, and I know you are a gentleman and lots of fun to travel with. What is the cost of the trip?"

"Do you mind paying half, $2,500?"

"I will have to make monthly payments to you since I only get my paycheck from Moscow at the end of each month."

On their drive to Sheridan, Wyoming, via Cheyenne, Wheatland, Casper, and Buffalo, John tells Lara, "I read an article in *Wikipedia* on Yellowstone National Park last night and found out there was a lot I did not know about the park. It was the first national park in the U.S., established in 1872, and is well known for its wildlife and geothermal features, especially Old Faithful geyser. Half of the world's geysers and hydrothermal features are in Yellowstone. Yellowstone Lake is one of the largest high-elevation lakes in North America and is centered over the largest super volcano on the continent. Hundreds of species of amphibians, birds, fish, mammals, and reptiles have been reported in the park. Visitors usually see in the beautiful forests and grasslands many antelope, buffalo, deer, and elk.

"Although we got to see our own bear, hopefully we can spot one from the car. As we drive around the park, we can also admire the lakes and waterfalls. I plan to show you Yellowstone Falls, the

Grand Canyon of the Yellowstone, Yellowstone Lake, and many other beautiful features of the park. Since we will be staying at the Old Faithful Inn for two nights, you will have several occasions to see the eruption of Old Faithful. The Continental Divide of North America goes through the southwestern part of the park. The origins of the Yellowstone and Snake rivers are near each other on opposite sides of the divide. The Yellowstone River is a tributary of the Missouri River that joins the Mississippi River that eventually empties into the Gulf of Mexico, while the Snake River joins the Columbia and drains into the Pacific Ocean.

"On my previous trips to Yellowstone, I flew from Denver to Jackson in the early morning, rented a car, and stayed one night in Jackson. In the afternoon, I usually took a nice stroll in the downtown area looking at shops, then had dinner. Early the next morning, I drove to Yellowstone with a stop to admire the beautiful Grand Tetons and take pictures. In Yellowstone, I always stayed at the Old Faithful Inn. After my two nights at the inn, I would drive through West Yellowstone to Idaho Falls to see friends then back to Jackson."

"It appears like this trip will certainly be a little different."

"Well, for one thing, I have a beautiful, intelligent, and 'fun to be with' professor to accompany me. I have only entered the park from the east side once, and it was years ago. To change the subject, as you know, I have been taking a class and studying how to fly a single-engine airplane. I would also like to parachute out of a plane strapped to a professional instructor. Would you like to join me in a tandem jump?"

"I will have to give that some thought since it sounds like one could have a heart attack jumping from the plane."

"We could find a handsome instructor to strap you to! Now I am reminded about a parachute story. President Nixon, Secretary of State Kissinger, and a boy scout are in a small government airplane. The plane develops engine problems, and the pilot tells everyone to parachute off the plane. However, there are only two parachutes, so the pilot says the president must be saved,

and Nixon takes one of the parachutes and jumps. The pilot tells
Kissinger that he should let the young lad jump, but Kissinger
says that he is the smartest man in the world and needs to be
spared. Then Kissinger jumps. The boy scout tells the pilot not
to worry about him. The smartest man in the world just grabbed
the backpack off my back and jumped. The second parachute is
over there."

They both have a good laugh as they pull into the Super
Eight Motel parking lot in Sheridan. Following their arrival and
check-in, they have a walk around the small town and end the
day with a Mexican dinner.

The couple leaves Sheridan after an early breakfast and
drive to Burgess Junction, Lovell, and Powell via HY-14A. Lara
is especially taken with the spectacular drive over a pass with
beautiful mountains into a valley with the Bighorn River. After
reaching Cody, they go back to Burgess Junction on HY-14
through Greybull and past the Shell waterfall. Following a short
visit to the Heart Mountain Barracks, which housed more than
fourteen thousand Japanese Americans during WWII, they go
onto Burgess Junction and then back to Cody on HY-14A. After
checking into the Six Gun Motel for two nights, they visit the
nearby dam above Cody that holds back Buffalo Bill Reservoir.
The dam was built in 1905–1910 and was the tallest in the world
in 1910. Later, they return to town for a walkabout. The town is
very lively.

They leave Cody early the next morning on HY-120 and
head northwest out of town. Several miles later, they turn onto
HY-296, which is Chief Joseph Scenic Highway. The drive is
breathtaking, with beautiful snowcapped mountains and rolling
green hills in view. After going through Cooke City, Montana,
they enter the northeast gate of Yellowstone National Park and
then to Tower Junction and Mammoth Hot Springs. On the drive
to Yellowstone Canyon, they spot a bear and take some pictures
from the car. Further on, they see many buffalo roaming the
hills and pastures. A little past the canyon, John parks Red and

walk to the lower falls of the Yellowstone River. Then they travel to Yellowstone Lake to catch HY-14 back to Cody. The highway parallels the Shoshone River and through a breathtaking canyon with weathered volcanic rocks that looks like towers and other interesting structures. The beauty lasts until the town of Wapiti and the Buffalo Bill Reservoir.

The next morning, they leave Cody early and enjoy the drive again through the beautiful canyon from Shoshone Reservoir, past Sleeping Giant ski area, to the east gate of the park. Not surprisingly, there are a lot of cars on the roads. Before reaching Fishing Bridge, they pass herds of buffalo and elk in the meadows. After lunch in the car, they arrive at the Old Faithful Inn. Lara especially likes the area. The discussion over dinner is mainly about what they did during the day and their plans for their last full day in the park. John asks Lara, "After seeing Old Faithful Geyser shoot off in the morning, how about heading to the western entry to the park and having a short walk around the downtown area of West Yellowstone? We can have a few stops to see some mud pots and maybe more buffalo and elk."

"That sounds great, John. I sure love this park."

After visiting West Yellowstone, they leave the park and enter Teton National Park. John starts making periodic stops for pictures of the beautiful Tetons. In Jackson, they stay at the Snow King Resort next to the ski area. After a long walk around the downtown, they have dinner in a restaurant that was once a movie theater. Lara tells John that someday she would love to come back in the winter and ski the slopes next to the lodge. John agrees. They end the day by buying some food to eat in the car the next day.

They leave Jackson before the sun came up and take HY-189 to Hoback Junction. John stops there for gas and tells Lara, "Take a look at this Wyoming/Colorado map and see the route we will take back home. We will first take HY-191 to Rock Springs. There, we will get on I-80 and go east through Rawlins. At Walcott, we will head south on HY-230 that changes to HY-125 at the

Colorado border. We will continue on the highway through Walden to Granby. Someday we can return to Walden and follow the highway that parallels the Poudre River to Fort Collins. It is a beautiful drive through the canyon. When we get to Granby, we will head east through Rocky Mountain National Park and stop in Estes Park for dinner. I think you will enjoy the scenery in the park and maybe see some wildlife. We will probably arrive home after dark."

Several days after their return to Pine Shadows, Lara sends an e-mail to her folks.

Dear Mom and Dad,

Since I wrote you last, summer vacation has started here, and John has given me some wonderful memories. We first went to Yellowstone National Park in Wyoming and got to see many of the remarkable things there, such as mud pots, geysers, and lots of buffalo and elk. We even saw a black bear. Of course, we have our own bear at Pine Shadows that I wrote you about in my last e-mail. The most exciting thing in my life occurred two days ago. John took me skydiving. We were each strapped to professional divers. As we were about to jump from the plane, I decided not to, but John held my hand as the four of us left the plane. After a minute or two, I opened my eyes to see the earth coming up on us fast, then the parachute opened, and we slowly glided safely back to Earth. I have never been so terrified and thrilled in my life. Next week, John is taking me on a National Geographic cruise part way up the western coast of Alaska. It should be exciting. I also want to tell you that following the cruise, we will be attending a conference in Sweden, and guess what, we plan to visit you both for almost a week. This will give you an opportunity of meeting the man I am in love with. Well, take care and give my love to my brother.

Love and miss you so much, Lara

The night before they left for Alaska, Lara read about one of John's trips to West Africa.

On Saturday, December 6, I left Denver on a nonstop Lufthansa flight to Frankfurt. Lufthansa Airlines has a good routine of boarding passengers from the back of the plane to the front. As usual, I was sitting near the back in an aisle seat with no one next to me. I started a conversation with the beautiful redheaded stewardess by first asking her if I could help her wash dishes. After she laughed and said no, thank you, I asked her where she was from. Joanna said that she was Irish but living in Frankfurt. She likes the city very much and has flown to most cities in the world where Lufthansa flies. We also talked about Belfast and the Titanic. *She did not like Belfast. This was her second time to Denver and did not give me a favorable impression of my native city. I told her that I was going to Equatorial Guinea. She said that Malabo is nice and safe. Then she excused herself since she had to assist some passengers with their luggage.*

The flight to Frankfurt was about eight hours on a Boeing 747. After landing the next morning, I stayed at the Park Inn hotel across from the airport for one night. On Monday morning, I returned to the airport for my flight to Malabo. Security was very tough. First, there was a long wait in line, then my bag was delayed going through X-ray with several officials coming over to examine the X-ray picture. Then about five minutes later, they physically went through the bag. Following this episode, I went to the Lufthansa airport lounge, where I got some free food and drink.

The plane ride to Malabo was five hours with an hour's stop in Abuja, the capital of Nigeria. Abuja is surrounded by mountains, and near the airport, one looked like Sugarloaf Mountain west of Boulder.

was half full of passengers that had flown out of a city on the mainland.

The plane left Malabo forty-five minutes early, and I realized I had almost missed the flight. After about an hour later, the plane landed in Libreville, and everyone got off the plane except me. I waited about an hour while the plane was being cleaned. Then the plane filled up with new passengers. I was lucky to have a window emergency row seat with the middle seat vacant. My travels so far had been with people speaking English, German, Spanish, and French. Now I could add Portuguese to the list.

After a sleepless five-hour flight, the plane landed in Casablanca, where there were no health or fever checks at the arrivals hall. After a little wandering around the airport, I saw a sign that read "Transit Hotel." I found out that the airline would provide a cost-free room at the nearby Relax Hotel as well as lunch. There, I got several hours' sleep.

While waiting for my flight to Banjul, I went to the airport restaurant so I could get a bite to eat. Near my table was a very strange guy. He kept moving his eyes and lips as if he was talking to someone. This kept up about twenty to twenty-five minutes until he left the restaurant.

My December 10 flight to Banjul left Casablanca at 10:00 p.m. and arrived in Banjul at 1:30 a.m. on Thursday, December eleventh. After flying about three hours, the plane made a short stop in Bissau, Guinea-Bissau. The landing strip was very rough and the airport is small with no jetways. The Republic of Guinea-Bissau, a small country in Western Africa, is one of the world's poorest nations, and the official language is Portuguese. Many people outside of Bissau speak only an indigenous language or Creole. The country's 1998–1999 civil war devastated the economy.

The Banjul airport is fairly nice and not too big. There was a driver from the Sheraton Hotel waiting in the arrivals hall but with a lady's name on his sign, not mine. The lady did not show, so I was the only one in the van. The drive to the hotel took about half an hour on a desolate road with few houses about. After check-in, as usual, I told the bellboy I could find the room okay as I did not want to tip him. But the hotel clerk insisted, and he was right. We got on the elevator and went down instead of up. The third floor was the reception, the second floor was the tour desk, the first floor was the main restaurant and breakfast room, and the zero floor the bar, beach, pool, and guest rooms. After leaving the elevator, we had a long walk that had stairs in some places, and the walkway changed directions three times. Later that day and the next, I still got lost in going back to the room. The first day, I slept until the last call for breakfast at 10:00 a.m., then I arranged for a two-hour tour.

My guide, Ibrahim, told me that Gambia's population is a mix of Christian and Muslim and that there are no religious problems. The Muslims celebrate Christmas, and the Christians celebrate Ramadan. Our first stop was south to a fishing village, where we had a walk around to see many fish for sale, boats, and ladies fixing fishnets. Ibrahim was not married but had a girlfriend. The driver had a wife and three young girls. Both guys were in their early forties and good-looking. There were many different types of small fishing boats on the beach. What was strange to see in the distance was a large modern windmill for power generation near a cell phone relay tower. We continued our southerly drive to a remote village, where our Land Rover drove down a path. We stopped at a grass-covered hut, where Ibrahim's grandmother lives. She was a very old and fragile-looking woman, and her twenty-year-old granddaughter was looking after her.

After that visit, we returned to the hotel about 1:00 p.m., where I got a wonderful massage. At four, I rejoined Ibrahim and the driver to go north into Banjul. On the way, we went through a very crowded town full of roadside shops selling everything anyone would want except we had no luck in finding a baseball hat. After slowly driving through the small town with much traffic, we got on the only four-lane road in the country. Before going over a bridge near the city, there was a police lady checking cars. The bridge goes over a waterway that connects a small tributary of the Gambia River with the Atlantic Ocean. The main part of the extremely wide Gambia is north of Banjul, and it divides the long narrow country in half. The entire country is surrounded by Senegal. By the way, one of the pleasures of the country is that most people speak English in addition to their native tongues of Wolof or Mandinka.

At the entrance to Banjul is a giant arch called July 22 Arch. We had a drive around, seeing lots of shops in front of and inside old and new buildings. Nothing to write home about. There was a new beautiful parliament building near the arch. Following the tour, we went back to the hotel.

From the balcony of my room, the view of the Atlantic Ocean and sandy beach was super. The five-star hotel is also great with each group of rooms spread out on a hillside. There is a very large swimming pool between the bar and the beach. Few people were at the hotel, about twenty, and Ibrahim said tourism was very depressed because of Ebola in neighboring Guinea, Sierra Leone, and Liberia. There were about a dozen lovely cats wandering around the hotel grounds. It looked like they had a great life. Only a yellow one would let me pet it. I was very impressed by the kind and friendly people, the great hotel, the fact that everyone spoke English, the wonderful, clean beaches and interesting villages and towns. I was told that crime is nonexistent in the country. I would rate the country as probably one of the safest and nicest African countries I have visited. I will recommend that the Stevens put this on their travel plan list.

On the flight from Banjul to Casablanca, which left about 2:00 a.m., Saturday, December 13, there was a stop at the Deparaia Nelson Mandela airport about 3:00 a.m. The city is on the island of Chegadas, which is near Sal Island, where I had had several visits to on my way back to the States from South Africa. The Deparaia airport is extremely small and the runway very short. On landing, I shot almost into the seat ahead of me. Now I know what it feels like to land on an aircraft carrier. The runway was used for both landings and takeoffs, and our departure was like being shot out of a canon. Almost all the passengers on the Boeing 737 with about two hundred seats got off in Dupraia, and only a handful came on. It was the emptiest flight of my flying days.

Prior to getting on the 8:00 p.m. Saturday Air Maroc flight to Yaounde, I again spent the day at the Relax Hotel near the airport as a guest of the airline. The hotel is new, but the tile floors transmit sounds from the room above, and it made for having no rest. The hotel provided breakfast and lunch, but as my first stay, there were no towels in the room, and the TV did not work.

The flight was about two hours late in departing Casablanca in the rain. Earlier at the boarding gate, everyone was shoving and pushing. I yelled out at one point, "We all have assigned seats!" Earlier, I made some sheep sounds, ba-ba. Once we got past the gate, we had to walk down some stairs to board buses and wait some more. Then the bus proceeded to the plane, but the driver got lost and circled around the airport once.

I was reminded during this trip, why so many of the people I have come into contact with, especially here in Africa, want to come to America to be American citizens. I am so thankful that my grandparents had the courage to leave their homeland with secure jobs and their relatives and make the hard journey across the Atlantic to a place

Kabiye are commonly spoken as well. Togo is a long narrow country paralleling Benin to the east, Burkina Faso to the north, and Ghana to the west. Lome is to the right of Benin to the south, and the population is about six million.

I arrived in Lome a little after noon, and my driver to the Ibis Hotel was waiting for me. There was a football team in the arrivals hall that was in the city to play a game. They had a trophy with them that the approximately ten players had won at their last city, assuming it was Yaoundé. On the roads, there were about an even number of cars and motorbikes and lots of horn honking. The city is very large, and there is a mixture of office buildings, no more than about ten stories high, and lots of other old and new buildings. In the outskirts of the city, there were nice big homes as well as shacks.

Later after check-in, I hired a taxi to have a ride to a supermarket, where I bought some junk food, and then went around the market places to try and find a baseball hat with Togo written on it. No one had one, and they said they had lost some type of championship, so the hats were not produced. It was interesting to drive around the small side streets with small shacks on the curb with their owners selling everything under the sun except for the hat I wanted. Trying to park and allow a lane of traffic through was quite a challenge for my driver, Aholu. Everyone seemed well dressed.

The Ibis appears to be about three-stars, much like a good Motel 6, and it faces the ocean to the south, and the beach is right across a four-lane main road. The harbor has many big ships anchored, and at night, they sure light up the bay. The hotel grounds are quite large with a big swimming pool out front with a bar

The sad news on the TV that night was the hostage taking in a café in Sydney, where after a seventy-two-hour standoff, the police broke in and killed the Muslim gunman. A woman and a man were also killed in the may lay.

The weather the next day was very humid and warm but with blue skies. In the afternoon, I had Aholu take me on a two-hour tour of the city. Aholu had a great surprise for me before we started the tour—he had found a baseball hat with Togo embroidered on the front. First, we went to the border with Ghana, just about a mile west of the hotel. Aholu warned me not to take any walks on the beach after sunset as there are guys with knives that will either kill you, rob you, or kidnap you and take you out by boat to one of the ships. We next went by Togo University, and the grounds are about one mile square. The nearby American Embassy has a big wall around it as does the university. Some of the roads we went on were full of potholes, and I was concerned about a blown-out tire and my waiting outside in the heat while Aholu changed the tire. Later, we caught a nice four-lane highway that seemed to go around the city to the port area. The port was very large with nearby tire and concrete block manufacturing and a large fish market. Aholu said that only the men were allowed to buy fish since the women bought the fish and resold them at a higher price. It seemed like everywhere we went, there were street-side shacks selling stuff, and at the stop signs or lights, mainly young boys were carrying many things to buy. Most women walking around had a tray of some type of goods on their heads. I wondered where all the buyers came from to purchase all the goods for sale.

The next morning, I went to the airport to catch my flight to Douala. However, I had to wait outside in the hot sun for twenty to thirty minutes before they would let us in. Meanwhile, I got very sick, and when I got to the check-in counter, the agent told me I only had a single-entry visa into Cameroon, and I had already used it on my visit to Yaoundé. I had planned to stay in Yaoundé for a couple of days before

*going to Benin City for a couple of nights then a night in
Lagos. However, it was good that I could not leave Lome
as I got sicker, probably food poisoning and heat stroke,
so I returned to the Ibis for two more nights. I recovered
a couple of days later, so I could catch my return flight via
Lagos.*

*I was surprised that there were not any health checks
in Houston airport as we had had at the African airports.
I arrived back in Denver at noon on the first day of winter.*

IV

After John and Lara left Red at a DIA parking lot and went
through airport security, they boarded an Alaska Airlines flight
to Seattle. In Seattle, they had a three-hour wait before their two-
hour flight to Juneau. The Juneau airport is small with five gates,
and the runway and taxi way are on the same road. At the airport,
they were met by Joseph, a National Geographic representative,
along with a dozen of their fellow passengers. He told the group,
"You have four hours to explore the capital of Alaska. It was here
in 1880 that Joe Juneau, Richard Harris, and Chief Keowa found
gold in one of the small creeks descending from the mountains,
touching off the first of the northern gold rushes. Today Juneau
is a small city of 3,200 inhabitants dedicated to administrating
the largest state in the nation. It is also the only state capital on
the continent that you cannot directly drive to from the other
U.S. state capitals."

The group first went by bus to Mendenhall Glacier, where they
had about a mile's walk to a large waterfall at the end of the trail.
After about an hour's visit to the glacier and falls, everyone was
bused back into town to spend about an hour walking around.
On the bus following the walk, John whispered to Lara that it was
indeed enough time to see the older part of the capital.

After arriving at Juneau's main dock and boarding the National Geographic ship, *Sea Bird*, the group joined about two dozen other passengers who had arrived earlier for a safety drill, appetizers, and introductions in the lounge, followed by dinner. John and Lara's cabin is between the lounge and the staff dining room on the lowest level of the three-level *Sea Bird*. The small cabin has a sink between two single beds. There is a bathroom shared with the cabin next door. It has a toilet and shower that shoots water over the bathroom when one takes a shower. The water exits through a drain in the middle of the floor.

After cruising south from Juneau, the *Sea Bird* went out of Stephen's Passage and into Holkham Bay during the night. Holkham Bay is the entrance to the majestic Tracy Arm-Fjords Terror Wilderness. This wilderness, established in 1980, is 653,180 acres in size and has Tracy and Endicott Arm Fjords in the center of it. Tremendous glaciers carved this spectacular fjord system deep into the heart of the coastal mountains of the mainland. It is here where the passengers spent the second day of the expedition, spending some time on shore and on ship.

On the ship, John saw Felex, the Russian sailor who was aboard the *Akademic Abraham*. John walked over to say hello to Felex, but he walked away from John without saying anything. John told Lara about the incident, the problems he had with him in the past, and his suspicions that Felex tried to kill him. John asked Lara if she would mind going to Felex and find out all she could about him since she could communicate with him in Russian.

After Lara met with Felex, she went back to their cabin and told John what she found out. "Felex told me that he got fired from his job on the *Akademic Abraham* because of accusations you made to the captain about him trying to kill you. He said that they were all false accusations but that he hoped that you would die on this voyage. John, I think you should beware of this big, mean-looking man."

John did not sleep well that night thinking about Felex. He thought that it was hard to dismiss three previous attempts on his life as accidents during trips to the Arctic, Antarctica, and Greenland.

Following breakfast, some of the passengers saw about a dozen seals, many small narrow waterfalls, a couple of big falls, and the glacier. Later, the group received a briefing from Joseph about the day's activities, which included spending the rest of the morning cruising through this spectacular fjord, looking for wildlife, sailing by icebergs, and getting a look at the glaciers that carved this amazing scenery. The group also received a short safety talk on how to behave if they encountered a brown or black bear. Joseph first stated, "You must always be in groups of five or more. If you see a bear approaching, do not run, but stay still and bunch up." A few minutes later, Joseph emphasized not to take any food along as it could attract bears from long distances.

After the meeting, Lara told John that he should have told everyone about the bear attack at Pine Shadows.

"You are right. During my bear attack, I should not have run but stood still and raised my hands. If that did not work, I should have dropped to my knees and prayed." Lara laughed.

"Lara, you heard Joseph advise everyone to be sure and not have any food with them. I wanted to say that everyone should be sure and brush their teeth before departing for the walk."

With a hug, Lara told John, "You are sure a comedian and lots of fun to be with. I love you so much."

"Lara my dear, I also love you very much."

After lunch, about half of the passengers went out on Zodiacs for about two hours to cruise the area while John, Lara, and the rest of the passengers went ashore for a walk.

On the walk, naturalist Macean was explaining to the group about each plant they came to for the first time. At one flower, he asked if someone would get down on their hands and knees and smell it. Of course, John volunteered and said it smelled like feces. McClean said, "Indeed it smells like shit and is called an outhouse lily." Later, the group came upon bear poop on the trail that was fresh. McClean told everyone not to worry as he was carrying along a spray can of turmeric to use on attacking bears.

After lunch, the *Sea Bird* made its way back out of Tracy Arm, with everyone enjoying the scenery that was missed in the early morning. Later in the afternoon, the ship anchored at Williams Cove. While most of the passengers were in their cabins resting, John was taking a stroll around the lower, narrow deck with Lara walking several feet behind him. As John was passing a doorway, a bucket full of soapy water was thrown in front of him that causes John to fall and slide under the railing into the sea. Lara screamed. A couple of crew members who witnessed the accident came to Lara with a life buoy, a ring-shaped, life-saving tube tied to a rope, and pulled John to safety. Lara said that she saw Felex throwing the water on deck. After John returned to their cabin and changed into some dry clothes, they went to the captain with their suspicion that Felex was trying to kill John. After Felex was summoned to join the three, he denied trying to kill John and said he just emptied the bucket of wastewater on deck not knowing anyone was there and returned to complete his work inside the ship.

At dinner, John and Lara shared a table with a spinal surgeon from Omaha and his wife, Grace. Dr. Mike Long was born and raised in Rwanda. He and John had a lot of talk about Africa, and the Longs had even spent considerable time in South Africa. Mike had a sister in Port Elizabeth that he saw about every three years on his visits to South Africa. Originally, he got his MD in Cape Town and then went to Canada, where he could not make a living as a surgeon. Then he and Grace moved to the United States. It was an enjoyable meal for the four of them.

The next morning, John and Lara woke up as the ship was in the beautiful little arm of Thomas Bay called Scenery Cove. After breakfast, they went on a hike with about a dozen others to Cascade Creek. Living up to its name, Cascade Creek has a roaring waterfall. The short hike went to the base of the falls, where most of the group got baptized by the mist of the waterfall. John, Lara, and a few other brave souls went to the top of the waterfall. They had a walk along a steep, slippery trail, followed by having to cross a nine-inch wooden blank across a ditch. One lady fell off and rolled over in the rain forest but was not hurt.

After lunch, the ship cruised over to Petersburg while the group heard a presentation by Steve Macean. Afterward, most of the passengers went ashore and visited the picturesque community of Petersburg (population 3,100) on Mitkof Island that was settled by Peter Buschmann at the turn of the century; this small town still shows off its Norwegian heritage. Fishing is the mainstay of the community, with approximately $22 million of seafood processed each year. Most of the group went on a walk along the docks to learn about fishing and fishing boats and later explored the town on their own. On the couple's walk around Petersburg, they had several pictures taken of themselves standing in front of a small wooden sailing ship that was next to Bojer Wikan Fisherman's Memorial Park, a most unusual place in the center of the fishery town.

Following dinner on the *Sea Bird*, there was a humpback whale sighting. The ship followed the large whale as it swam alongside, surfacing every five to ten minutes with its tail flipping out of the water most of the time. Later, the couple had some great entertainment in their cabin, watching a beautiful sunset through their cabin window, along with the whale putting on a great close-in show.

Later, Lara pulled back the covers on John's bed and screamed. John darted out of the bathroom to find a large brown spiker, which he thought was a tarantula, on his bed. John captured the spider in a trash can, covered the can with a plastic bag, and took the spider to the bridge. The captain told the couple that they had never had anything like that on ship before, no snakes, rats, or mice. He summoned Macean to come to the bridge to have a look at the spider.

After Macean arrived and inspected the spider, he said, "It is a wolf spider, the largest one I have ever seen, and it can be found anywhere on land. As you see, they are like a hairy tarantula, only maybe not so big but still equally as scary. Their large size makes them generally feared. They are known to deliver a painful bite when handled, but their venom is not medically dangerous to humans. Given their size, one can imagine the fangs are also proportionately large, adding to the pain of a bite."

The captain said, "Macean, please take it ashore tomorrow, and let it loose."

After returning to their cabin, John and Lara discussed the incident. They both agreed that Felex brought the spider aboard and put it in John's bed.

After traveling through the night, the *Sea Bird* arrived at Chatham Strait at first light. Before breakfast, the ship cruised by scenic Red Bluff Bay of Baranof Island, and everyone got to see a brown bear with two cubs on shore. During breakfast, the *Sea Bird* headed north, stopping at Warm Springs Bay to pick up Andy Sabo from the Alaska Whale Foundation. Andy traveled with the group all morning, answering questions about whales, while most of the folks looked for the beautiful creatures in the water.

In the afternoon, the ship anchored at Hanus Bay next to Baranof Island. There is a well-maintained scenic trail on the island that goes through the forest, and everyone had an opportunity to hike toward Lake Eva. The forest on the island is particularly lovely, with a rich understory of mosses, ferns, and shrubs. The full cycle of forest life can be observed there with fungi-consuming dead trees, saplings rising from nurse logs, mature trees soaring into the canopy, and snags leaning over the small river. Everyone agreed it was a great walk.

When the couple woke up the next morning, the *Sea Bird* was sailing south into Idaho Inlet, a serene and lovely area, on the north side of Chichagof Island. The ship's anchor was dropped at a site known as Fox Creek, and it was there that the passengers spent the morning. Before breakfast, most of the passengers received a grand show from several killer whales and humpbacks. John got a great picture of two killer whales together. Later, a hike along the creek and through the forest was taken by everyone. The trails were made by wildlife, especially bears. The visitors saw some fresh bear poop, bear prints in the mud, and some scratch marks on a few trees. They had to cross a couple of small creeks on the scenic walk. The flora and fauna were wonderful to admire.

On Wednesday morning, the group had another great hike through the rainforest. In the afternoon, they went on a two-hour Zodiac cruise, through an area known as the Inian Islands, in rough waters. The Inian Islands are near where the Pacific Ocean comes into the northern end of the inside passage. It is a biologically rich area. Sea lions and seals are often plentiful there as well as seabirds, bald eagles, and muffins. The group saw quite a few sea lions, and one had caught a fish, and some others were trying to get the fish out of his mouth—it was quite a show. John got some great pictures. After dinner, the ship cruised in the area near Point Adolphus, just south of Glacier Bay National Park.

On Thursday, most of the group listened to a talk by one of experts aboard about Capt. George Vancouver, who cruised by what is now the entrance to Glacier Bay in 1794; he found it to be filled with a tidewater glacier. In 1879, when John Muir visited the same area, the glacier had retreated about thirty miles north into the bay. Today those same glaciers have retreated a total of sixty miles in a little over two hundred years and left behind a huge bay that is now protected as Glacier Bay National Park and Reserve. It is also designated as a World Heritage Site and a Biosphere Reserve.

The *Sea Bird* spent the entire day cruising the length of the west arm of the bay, stopping at places where the passengers got to view seabird nesting islands, beautifully exposed geologic formations, and, of course, the faces of the glaciers themselves. Along the way, they saw a couple of bears, mountain goats along the beaches, rocky headlands, and glacial outwashes. At the head of the bay, the ship lingered in front of Margerie Glacier, and the folks on deck got to see some calving. Masaki Shima, a park ranger/interpreter, and Alice Hald, a cultural heritage guide from Alaska Native Voices, came on board to discuss the area with the passengers.

The end point was Margerie Glacier. Next to Margerie was the Grand Pacific Glacier, which was covered in rock and was brown on top instead of white. After reversing course, the ship went back and stopped at Johns Hopkins Glacier. The passengers also got to see nine other tide water glaciers in the park.

After glacier watching, the *Sea Bird* stopped at the small town of Gustavus with an airport. The dock is next to the visitors' center, where most of the visitors had about a two-hour visit. John, Lara, and a few new friends took a walk past a nice campground and back to the lodge. Near the lodge was a display of a whale skeleton. The whale was named Snow.

On Friday, after traveling south through the night, the ship anchored during breakfast at Iyoukeen Cove on Chichagof Island. In 1902, this area was the site of a gypsum mine. The pilings along the shoreline are the only easy way to find remnants of the wharf that extended into deep water to load the ships with gypsum. Today the forest has reclaimed the area. Their hike began on a tidally exposed beach and continued along a wildlife trail just inside the forest. It was not a well-maintained trail, so the hikers had a little exploration.

In the afternoon, the ship started working its way south toward Peril Strait and Sergius Narrows for arrival in Sitka in the morning. Along the way, most of the passengers kept a watch for wildlife with some stops for viewing the animals.

At breakfast on Saturday, the *Sea Bird* docked in Sitka on Baranof Island. Sitka is the fourth largest city in Alaska with a population of almost nine thousand. Originally inhabited by the Tlingit Indians, the name Sitka comes from Shee Atika, the Tlingit name for the town. In 1804, Sitka became the capital of

Russian America and was renamed New Archangel. In 1867, Sitka was the location for the transfer of Alaska from Russian to United States ownership. Most of the visitors took a tour of the Raptor Rehabilitation Center, the Sitka National Historic Park, and St. Michael's Russian Orthodox Cathedral. Lara especially enjoyed their time in the Russian church that was full of gold figures, crosses, and statues.

In the afternoon, most of the passengers took a flight to Seattle. In Seattle, John and Lara transferred to a flight to Denver. After their arrival at Pine Shadows, Lara gave John a loving hug and thanked him for a wonderful trip.

With a kiss, he told Lara that he would like to marry her once the threat for his life was managed.

"John, you are such a dear man. I love you, and of course, I want to be your wife as soon as possible."

"Lara, just be sure that you want to marry a guy whose last three wives were murdered because of him."

"I love you so much and would die for you."

After another long kiss, they departed for their living quarters. A minute later, John called out, "Lara, your cost of the trip is your birthday and Christmas gifts."

"Thank you so much, John. Good night."

Chapter 4
Trips around the World

I

On their flight to Stockholm via London, John suggests to Lara that she may want to read in his diary about a trip to the Scandinavian countries that he took years ago. "The story may give you a glimpse of what we will see in Sweden."

I left Denver late on Friday afternoon, on a nine-hour nonstop flight to Frankfurt in a Boeing 747. On the flight, I met Autumn, who lives in Orange County, California, and travels a lot for a construction company. She was interesting to talk with. Later, I watched a good movie, Money Monster, *with George Clooney. After my arrival the next morning, I checked in at the Park Inn Hotel, near the Frankfurt airport, which is next to a nice park. I had a walk about the park later, and the weather was warm. The next morning at ten, I flew to Helsinki in two hours. After my arrival, I went to the city by train. The ride was thirty minutes and cost me five euros. (Finland uses the euro unlike the other Scandinavian countries.) The train went by many small hills covered with beautiful evergreen trees and made several stops at small communities. There is a big square in front of the main train station where I caught a taxi to the Hotel Arthur. My room was terrible for napping as a basketball court was directly above my room on the ninth floor.*

The next morning, I went to the International Conference on Nuclear and Radiochemistry. The conference was held in a nice building on the marina, with lots of big rocks around it and a couple of cruise ships anchored. There were 350 participants from thirty-four countries at the meeting. I happily met some American, Czech, German, and Russian friends. I also got to make some new friends. Everyone I met spoke English. I got caught up on some of their activities over lunch.

I left the meeting later in the afternoon and had a walk around some of the city. There were separate lanes for bikes and pedestrians, but still, I almost got hit twice by a bike. I took a hop-on, hop-off bus tour of the city and saw many buildings with unique architecture. Some of the places we stopped at and viewed on the bus tour were Senate Square, Olympia Ship Terminal, Swedish Theatre, Market Square, Rock Church, Parliament House, Helsinki Cathedral, and Uspenski Cathedral. That evening, a few friends and I ate at Malones Pub and listened to a band playing a variety of music.

On Tuesday, I took a boat tour on the Helsinki canal. The boat went by Korkeasaari Zoo, Kulosaari Building, Degero Canal, and many cottages on the islands. We also went through the narrow Degero Canal, where the boat hit the canal banks several times, and by Suomenlinna Sea Fortress and Vallisaari Hill with an old building on top. The two-hour ride around Helsinki was interesting. Afterward, I repeated the hop-on, hop-off bus ride I had taken yesterday. The city has several big and beautiful churches. There were only a handful of passengers on both the tour boat and bus. The weather was cold and rainy with sun in the afternoon. Later, I took the train to the airport to get my boarding passes for tomorrow morning's flights.

After checking out of the hotel the next morning, I took the train to the Helsinki airport. The airport is big but with no moving stairs. My SAS flight to Oslo took an hour, first flying over a broad river and flat land with lots of trees and lakes and then over dozens of small islands. At the Oslo airport, I took a flight to Kirkenes, about one and a half *hours of flying. There were some trees and lots of rocks near the airport. The landing was wild, with the plane breaking fast on a short runway. The airport is small with only four gates. At both airports, there were no jetways or stairs but ramps from the planes to the ground. Kirkenes is small with no bank at the airport to exchange money (8 kroner equals to $1). The bus at the airport went into town and called out stops, one of which was my hotel.*

I was staying at the Scandic Hotel, which was okay, but I had lunch at a better hotel on the marina, which was called Restaurant 69° Nord. It was a beautiful sunny day, and I only needed a light jacket. The city has a population of three and a half thousand. There used be a lot of mining here, but that has stopped, and now fishing and the service industry are the main income sources. The harbor area is nice with surrounding hills covered in what looks like aspen or birch trees, which are turning yellow already. I took a twenty-minute walk around the dock area, where I will board the MS Loften *at noon tomorrow.*

At eleven on Thursday, September first, a Hurtigruten cruise company bus collected me and my fellow passengers at various hotels and took us to the ship. It was cold and rainy, Thursday, September first. A big cruise ship that left today was with the same company, Hurtigruten, that our ship belongs to and is called Kong Harold. *Our ship, the MS* Loften, *was built in 1964 and is the smallest of Hurtigruten's twelve cruise ships. The ship has 150 beds, and there are about the same number of passengers aboard. I was told that the ship, which also serves as a merchant ship, usually docks at thirty-four ports. Most of the stops take only fifteen to thirty minutes to take on and off cargo, mail, and passengers. We left port at 12:30 p.m., and I got settled in my small cabin that I had all to myself. The cabin has one single bed, a place to hang clothes, and a sink. The toilets and showers are down the hall.*

Our first stop was in Vardo. Vardo is Norway's eastern port and is situated on the island of Vardoya with an underwater tunnel linking the island to the mainland. I had an hour's walk around the small village and visited an old fortress. The ship then proceeded in and out of Fjords as the land started to get more mountainous with some topped with snow; I even saw a couple of glaciers.

On September 2, the ship made a two-hour stop at Hammerfest, the world's most northernly town. The ship docked right in the town center, and I had a walk around the town that had a beautiful church. One could also walk up the hill overlooking the town, but I passed that experience up. There is also the Meridian Column in Hammerfest; it commemorates the first precise measurement of the earth, and the achievement was so important that it has become a UNESCO World heritage site. The ship next proceeded down the coast and made short stops at Oksfjord, Skjervoy, and Tromso. The Northern Lights were visible about ten. Of course, I had been taking lots of pictures.

The next day, the MS Loften *made a stop in Harstad and later went through Risoyrenna, which has a three-mile dredged channel. The ship made a short stop there as well as in Scortland, which is the main town in the region of Vesteralen and headquarters of the North Norwegian Coast Guard. At 2:20 p.m., the* Loften *stopped in Stokmarknes, where I took an hour's walk around town. Several additional passengers boarded the ship before our departure. We continued our trip by going through the strait of Raftsundet. We next went to Trollfjorden, and after departing, I had my usual 6:00 p.m. dinner at a table of four with Kate from Australia and two ladies from Boston. Both are retired, whereas Kate is a physiotherapist taking a month off work. Our next stop was Svolvaer, where I explored the town for two hours; there is an ice gallery and war museum there.*

On Sunday, we had a long stop in Bode at 2:30 a.m., but of course, I was asleep. At seven, there was a short stop in Ornes, but I did not get up until nine. Fifteen minutes later, we crossed the Arctic Circle and went by Vikingen island displaying a large globe outside, indicating the position of the town and the Arctic Circle. A little later, there was an Arctic Circle ceremony in the ship's bar, where everyone had a spoon of fish oil. At eleven, we had a short stop in Nesna and, at half past noon, a longer stop in Sandnessjoen, where I took a short walk. Downtown Sandnessjoen has a nice five-block walking street lined with a variety of shops. At lunch on ship, a couple from New Zealand joined me and the three ladies. Steven is a retired construction manager who has worked in many countries. His wife is a retired schoolteacher. The couple is traveling around the world for six months and spent a month traveling around Russia. They plan on driving from Florida to Colorado then to the Grand Canyon and California. After visits to Cuba and several South American countries, they will go by container ship home. Steven and his wife have found the less expensive ways to travel. After the ship departed Sandnessjoen, the scenery changed from hills with few trees to high mountains covered with many trees, mainly evergreens. I saw lots of narrow waterfalls coming off the tops of some of these mountains as well as many fjords; we were always close to shore.

Our next stop was Bronnoysund, where I had an hour's walk. The small city center has only one main street of five blocks, with a few restaurants and shops, and three small hotels. After departing Bronnoysund, the ship went into the rough open sea, and I had trouble sleeping during the night on the rocking vessel.

Monday morning, September 5, we visited an island with a fortress called Munkholmen then Trondheim, where I had a two-hour walk around the city. Trondheim was founded *by the Viking king Olaf Tryggvason in 997. It is Norway's third largest city with a population of 180,000. The most impressive thing was Nidaros Cathedral, where three queens and seven kings had been crowned. The city has a McDonald's and two Burger Kings. I loved the architecture of many of the old buildings.*

Later, after we left Trondheim, there was a short stop in Kristiansund that is situated on three islands. People have lived around this harbor for at least eight thousand years. The town has about 22,500 inhabitants. At five, the ship started crossing Hustadvika, an open stretch of sea, and arrived in Molde at nine for a forty-five-minute cargo change.

On our last day at sea, I had breakfast with a German student studying biology, an oil field engineer working for GE, and his Norwegian wife, who is a captain on a ferry. The engineer finds the oil, and his wife uses it! Tuesday was cold and rainy. At lunch, I sat with a couple from the United Kingdom, a man from France who looked like a terrorist, and Kate. We arrived in Bergen in the late afternoon. I then took a bus to the Best Western Sandviken Hotel on the edge of the nice downtown area. I need to return here someday to have more time to explore this beautiful city.

The next morning, I took a taxi to the airport. On the way to the airport, we went through several long tunnels. The airport is surrounded by mountains as is Bergen, with lots of evergreen trees on the mountains and in the valleys. The Bergen airport is nice with thirty gates. An hour later, I was at the gate to take a SAS flight to Visby via Stockholm. The flight to Stockholm was a little over an hour. Stockholm airport (Arlanda Airport) is huge with five terminals and a sky city, which is a giant shopping center.

Now I am on a two-engine turbo prop plane with four rows for my one-hour flight to Visby. Out of the plane's window, I saw many fjords, small and large lakes, and lots of evergreen forests and farms. I was sitting next to a sixteen-year-old high school student from Norway. She is on a national team to play Sweden in a soccer play-off game in Visby.

Visby is on the Swedish island of Gotland and is south of Stockholm. Gotland is a good-size island with about seventy thousand inhabitants, with half of them living in Visby. There, I stayed at the Best Western Solhem Hotel. After check-in, I took a walk around the inside of the old stonewalled city, which is quite large. The church is in the town square. Later, a parade of Ford Mustangs passed in the square next to the outdoor restaurant where I was having dinner. It is a wonderful city full of old ruins, one huge church, and many old buildings. I was happily surprised to come to such a historic and beautiful town. The people who live inside the walls can say that they live in a World Heritage City. Scattered inside the walled village are many old church ruins, including Stora Torget, St. Clemens, St. Nicolaus, St. Maria, St. Hans-Skolan, and St. Hans's ruins.

I took a one-and-a-half hour bus ride from Visby to Burgsvik. The land is flat with evergreen forests and dairy cow and sheep farms. As the bus got near Burgsvik, there were many farms and homes that had stone or rock walls built around them. I only had an hour to explore Burgsvik before the bus returned to Visby. The trip was worth it, however, since the lovely town, next to the ocean, had lots of beautiful old buildings.

On the morning of September 9, I got to the airport via shuttle bus in ten minutes for my six forty-five flight to Stockholm. The "Next Jet" flight to Mariehamn from Stockholm only had a dozen passengers, whereas the plane from Visby to Stockholm was fully loaded. This plane could hold thirty-three passengers. In Mariehamn, I stayed at the four-star Myfidelio Hotel Savoy. The city is very modern with many new buildings. I thought the island was part of

Sweden and paid the taxi driver in Swedish NOK, but they use euros since Aland Islands is part of Finland. Aland is an archipelago and self-governing with no army, but Finland owns the place.

I took a bus ride to the southern part of the city then another bus ride to the north side. The city is not too big. Next, I got on a bus that took me to the middle of the main island in thirty minutes, and I had to change buses in Godby. Then it took another half hour to get to Geta, on the north shore of Aland Islands. The return trip was directly back to Mariehamn, about thirty miles. The island is very much like Gotland, flat with fields of forest between farms. Some farms were growing apples, and others had sheep and dairy cows. The weather both days on Aland was great. I only needed my light jacket.

After a late breakfast on Saturday, I walked a block down to the three-block pedestrian walkway that had shops and restaurants. After the walkway, I took a long walk down to the north side of the city, where there is a fjord or marina with a sailing ship parked next to a museum. The other bay area is in the other direction, about two blocks from the pedestrian walkway. I had a pizza lunch at the Kino nightclub's pizzeria. After lunch, I had a nice discussion with the waitress, a good-looking blonde about twenty-one. She asked me if I was an American, and I said yes, and she said she was too. The young lady told me that she came here when she was thirteen to meet her father for the first time. Her father had divorced her mother a year after her birth in California. She finished high school here and learned Finnish. Her dad owns a car wash. The young lady has worked at various jobs and wants to be an artist. She plans to visit her mother for the first time since she left the U.S.

On Sunday, after a late breakfast at ten, I watched the TV news for a while. Later, I went on an hour-long walk *along the bay and then through the ship museum. During my time here, I saw at least a dozen old classic American cars, including a blue 1966 Chevrolet Impala, just like the one I once owned.*

I left the hotel at 4:00 p.m. for my 6:30 p.m. flight to Stockholm. The airport is small with only one departure gate. I found out at boarding time that my flight was canceled. During this time, I had befriended two fellow passengers, students from South Korea. They were exchange students studying in Stockholm. One was extremely beautiful. We were all bused to the Hotel Pommern, a block away from the Savoy Hotel, and I had dinner with the two young ladies. A fellow from Slovenia joined us, and he was quite interesting. The young man is a coach for an ice hockey team, and he was wearing a T-shirt with Slovenia printed on the front with the word "love" in bold letters. He said that his country name is the only one with love. He had come over on a ferry from Stockholm and got off at a remote dock, where there was no one around. He ended up thumbing a ride and was picked up by a fellow from Croatia. They had a lot to talk about on the way into Mariehamn. After finishing dinner, I said my goodbyes to the girls and the Slovenian and took a thirty-minute taxi ride to the ferry terminal in Langhashamn. I boarded the ferry at one in the morning. The Viking Line ferry was huge. It had ten decks with a restaurant on the top deck. I closed the evening by watching couples dancing to the great music of a band. There was also a pool, game room, and big duty-free shop. It was my first ride on a gigantic cruise ship that reminded me of the MGM Grand Hotel in Las Vegas. I liked it very much despite only getting a couple of hours sleep.

We arrived at 6:30 a.m. in Stockholm, and from there, I caught a taxi to the airport for my flight to Copenhagen. I finally got out of Copenhagen at 11:30 a.m. for a half-hour flight on a Danish Air transport plane (fully loaded) *to Ronne, Bornholm (part of Denmark). I had to pay $100 for the ticket since I had no reservation. (I decided at the last minute to take this adventure.) From the airport, I had a ten-minute drive to the nice and big Griffen Spa Hotel. The hotel overlooks the ocean across from a main road into the harbor area, about a ten-minute walk. Farther away from the ship area is old town and a shopping district about ten blocks long, with several outdoor restaurants. Bornholm Island has forty thousand inhabitants and no university. The first church in Ronne was built around 1275. It was later expanded and built from carved Gotland limestone. The church was renamed Church of Skt. Nicolai. It is a beautiful white building near the town center and close to the marina.*

I caught a bus, number 6, from the bus station near the city center and took it to the other side of the island, the east side, about a twenty-mile ride. The bus was almost full of school kids, probably high school, and a few of them exited the bus at numerous stops until we got to where only a few passengers remained on board. It is a beautiful island, and the road paralleled the ocean about half the time. The bus went through the following major towns: Arnager (airport), Aakirkeby, Nexo, Svaneke, Ostermarie, Aarsballe, and Knudsker. The countryside outside of the towns was mostly farms of hay, corn, and cows. Following the bus ride, I was thanking my guardian angels on how the right bus had come along first, how I had a terrific ferry trip, and just the right amount of time on this beautiful island.

At six on Tuesday morning, September 13, I was on my way to Copenhagen. The flying time from Bornholm to Copenhagen was thirty minutes. I had a two-hour wait in both Copenhagen and Helsinki airports. Both flights to Helsinki and Kemi Tornio were one and a half hours each. Kemi airport is small with one runway for takeoffs and landings. Kemi-Tornio is in Lapland. Upon arrival, taxi ride, and hotel check-in, I had a couple of hours walk around the small downtown area of Kemi. The large church in the town square is very unusual as it is pink. There is a large Second World War Monument nearby.

On Wednesday, I took the bus from Kemi to Oulu at a cost of five euros. There was a car and minibus accident along the way; an ambulance took away two people. A nice bike lane paralleled the highway. On the drive, there were lots of signs with moose pictures on them as well as many wind-powered mills, lakes, and trees on the flat landscape. The bus went through several small towns. The ride was about a hundred miles and took almost two hours.

I had a half-hour walk around the small downtown area of Oulu and took a few pictures, notably of the city hall and cathedral. At one, I took the train back to Kemi. The ticket cost was fifteen euros. The train route paralleled the highway that I had taken from Kemi. Kemi has two nice marinas, and from there, I could see two islands nearby. There are many shops, three massage parlors, and two big grocery stores in town. I had dinner at Subway.

At eight on Thursday morning, I was on a flight out of Kemi that landed half an hour later at the Helsinki airport in thick fog. I then took a flight to Oslo and had a long wait at the Oslo airport (five hours) for my flight to Alborg. After arriving at a nice and new airport in Aalborg (eleven gates), I took a short taxi ride to the Best Western hotel. The hotel was built in 1906 and has the old type of elevator. My room has squeaky floors. Later, I had a walk about the city that has a population of 160,000. There are nice bike paths between the streets and pedestrian walks. Next to the hotel is the Madorcu Bar. There were many college students going from bar to bar and meeting up with other college friends. It looked like some of the students were trying to pull a variety of pranks on their friends. One that I saw was four guys lying on the sidewalk with their mouths open while their buddies gave them wine via a cork on a string. Some of the students were in a variety of costumes.

On Friday morning, September 16, I went to the train station, a block from the hotel, to catch a train going to Frederikshavn at nine. The train had three cars, and there were two stops in Aaburg's subdivisions and several on the way in small towns. The land was flat, and there were many farms, mainly wheat, corn, and dairy cows. There were also several groves of wind-powered mills. It is a beautiful countryside. At ten, we stopped in Hjorring, and most of the passengers got off, including a large group of grade schoolers. I also saw a lady pushing a baby carriage built for four children, and sure enough, there were four youngsters in the carriage. The train arrived in Frederikshavn at half past ten. The trip was about forty miles.

I had a nice two-hour walk around the small city that has a nice marina with a docked ferry boat, a beautiful big church, and more than a dozen pedestrian-only streets lined with a variety of stores and restaurants.

I caught the 12:30 p.m. train back to Aalborg that continued all the way to Copenhagen. After my arrival back in Aalborg, I walked into a park on the opposite side of the train station from my hotel. The park is unusual as it has monuments with entertainers' names on them and the date they performed at the adjoining concert hall. Furthermore, each marker had a speaker, and one could push a button on the black plastic monument and hear one of the performer's songs. Some of the performers were Tom Jones, Harry Belafonte, Rod Stewart, Dionne Warwick, and Elton John. I then continued my walk to the other side of the city center and discovered three long pedestrian walkways lined with shops and restaurants. In one area, there were old pubs in various old buildings with various groups of college kids celebrating the start of classes. A wide fjord was nearby with a couple of ships docked. Next to the marina was a park full of college kids. On the way back to the hotel, I spent an hour at a massage parlor, getting some relief for my tired feet.

One thing that I liked so far on the trip was that most of the ladies were blonds and good-looking, and I did not see any panhandlers. Well, I thought there was one, and I got embarrassed: I saw an old lady sitting and holding a coffee cup. So I walked up to her with change in my hand and asked the lady if she wanted some money. As she said, no thanks, in English, I noticed that there was a little coffee in the cup. It also appeared like everyone in Scandinavia prefers to use credit cards instead of cash for everything, including taxi and vending machines.

On Saturday, September 17, I took a taxi to the Aalborg airport for my 10:30 a.m. flight to Copenhagen, followed by a flight to Frankfurt, then home.

II

Early on Saturday morning, an Uber driver arrived at Pine Shadows in his black BMW to take John and Lara to Denver International Airport. The middle-aged driver did most of the talking on the drive. He told the couple that he worked full time for United Airlines as a baggage handler. "It is hard work, but I do receive free flights around the country. My next trip will be to Hong Kong then Shenzhen, China."

The ride took about an hour. After the couple got through security, they went to the United Airlines lounge, where they had a free breakfast. Their flight was supposed to leave for Chicago at 10:30 a.m., but when John looked at the information display for departures, it was delayed several hours because of the hurricane in Houston. John then grabbed Lara, and they left the lounge in a hurry to try and get on a flight to Chicago that was boarding. When they got to the gate, John found out that the flight was full. They then went to the United Airlines business desk to try to get to Gothenburg another way. They ended up on a Lufthansa flight that was leaving for Munich at 4:00 p.m. instead of their planned route through Frankfurt that then went nonstop to Gothenburg. Thus, they spent about four hours in the United lounge, where they had a nice lunch. While they enjoyed more free food and drinks, Lara told John, "I sent my folks an e-mail when we would arrive Moscow. I also wrote about our wonderful trip to Alaska. When will we arrive in Gothenburg?"

"We leave for Munich at three, and after our arrival tomorrow morning, we will take a two-hour flight to Stockholm then another flight to Gothenburg, arriving in Gothenburg early tomorrow afternoon."

On the transatlantic flight, John watched a couple of movies, and Lara read more of John's travels in his diary.

I left Denver via Atlanta for Johannesburg on May 11, arriving the next day after a fourteen-hour flight. I stayed at the Hotel Grand one night before flying to Cape Town. There, I rented a car, and suffering from jet lag, I somehow managed to drive on the wrong side of the N-2 highway, along with trying to operate the gearshift with my left hand. Another problem was that I kept turning on the windshield wipers to turn since the turn signal lever was on right. On the way, I passed lots of beautiful rolling hills of farmland, some covered with grapes, sheep, and cattle, with beautiful mountains in the background. There were also a few wineries as I drove by Stellenbosch. The drive was about five hours, and the road from the N-2 highway to Stilbaai was sixteen miles; it started to rain during the last few miles.

Upon arrival, Bret, Elda, and their son came to the car to greet me. I thought to myself that they have not changed a bit and do not complain about old-age joint pains. Jan is eighty and is still dyeing his hair black. Their home has been added onto twice since my last visit with Margrit. The home has four bedrooms, two bathrooms, a den, a kitchen, a two-car garage, and large living and dining rooms. On Saturday, Bret showed me the local highlights around the coast with its beautiful bay area. That night, Elda fixed a steak dinner and had a friend over from her local writing club, Carol. She had just moved into a new patio home nearby overlooking the ocean. Her brother wanted her late mother's home, where she had moved from, so she sold it so he could have half the proceeds. Carol earns a living as a massage therapist. She is divorced and has a son and two grandchildren living in Cape Town, a daughter with children in Johannesburg, and a single daughter in Australia.

The next day, Carol joined us for Mother's Day brunch at a nearby game lodge, and then we took a two-hour safari drive and saw two elephants, three giraffes, and three lions. The highlight was that one of the lionesses chased our safari vehicle and almost caught up with us. The ride was very windy and cold but no rain. That night, Carol gave me a wonderful massage at her place.

The next morning, I left after breakfast to drive to the Cape of Good Hope. About halfway, I had some excitement on the N-2 highway. I was traveling the speed limit of seventy miles per hour, and as I was going around a blind curve, I encountered a troop of baboons crossing the road. I barely missed hitting a couple of them. It was a shocking and scary event.

I had beautiful weather all the way to Cape Town. Before going to the airport, I drove around the park at the Cape of Good Hope and watched several baboons jump from car to car in the parking lot. One guy had to wait to get in his car as a large baboon was taking a nap on the top of his car. Later, I caught my flight to Johannesburg and again stayed at the Hotel Grand.

After a big and wonderful breakfast at the hotel the next morning, I went to the airport by taxi. There, I had a good walk around the airport and went into a shop called Out of Africa. Tears came to my eyes as I felt the presence of Margrit. She had loved this shop and used to spend a lot of time there as we waited for flights on past visits to South Africa. The flight to Antananarivo left at ten for about three hours of flying. Madagascar is an hour ahead of South African time.

Madagascar is one of those destinations that seem to conjure up a thousand images just upon hearing the name alone. It is exotic and little known and is an island filled with strange and exciting flora and fauna. It is truly a land of beautiful landscapes with diverse features and astounding natural beauty. From the craggy eroded sandstone sculptures of Isalo National Park and the stunning coastline of the west to the rolling hills of the south and the seemingly prehistoric forests of the dramatic Tsaranoro Valley, Madagascar's beauty is certainly inspiring. Being cut off from the African mainland for millions of years has resulted in a diverse number of endemic species found nowhere else on Earth. Of these, the lemurs have attracted special interest, and there are many different types. Madagascar is also rich in birdlife with many endemic species, and there are also several unique reptile species, including the amazing chameleon.

The South African Airways plane landed in Antananarivo a little after noon, and I took a taxi to the Capital Hotel. The driver was very accommodating and took a few detours to show me some significant sights in the city, like the Parliament House and the Pyramids (as they are called) housing a tomb of one of their presidents. In the distance, there were beautiful mountains, and one resembled a pyramid. The city is very spread out with lots of wide open spaces, but I did see concentrated housing on some of the distant hills. The hotel sits across from a large hotel the Chinese are building and is next to government houses, parliament, and the presidential house.

I spent all of Wednesday in the city. I took a city tour and visited the Ministry of Environment and the University, which overlooks the city in all directions. Most of the people seem very friendly, and I saw no beggars. The school children love to get their pictures taken and to see the taken picture. There appears to be a lot of Asian influence here. Car drivers are very polite, and there was no horn honking, even though traffic was slow and voluminous. There was roadwork going on in one place that caused a big delay, but drivers continued to be very courteous. Later, cars were held up while a long presidential entourage drove out with lots of police around; the newspapers that morning read that he was going to a political rally that day. Apparently, they are having elections just like in South Africa.

At the Antananarivo airport for my return to Johannesburg, I met three American girls who had spent three months there helping the needy people. They all go to different universities in the east, and one girl was from Colorado. There were also about ten guys with an American church group who had spent some time in Madagascar, also helping the people.

When leaving Madagascar, the skies were clear, but over Africa, it was very hazy. I returned to Johannesburg about six and, after a couple of hours later, caught my flight back to the U.S.

Over dinner, Lara told John that she sure enjoyed reading about his trip to South Africa and Madagascar. "You were very brave in driving the rental car on the wrong side of the road."

"I suggest that you read about my trip to a couple of the Pacific Islands, where I also drove rentals."

Following their dinner, John resumed watching movies, and Lara read about some of his trips to the South Pacific Islands.

On my last night in Sydney, I had dinner at KFC and then returned to the hotel to make an early night of it since I had arranged a taxi to pick me up at four in the morning for my flight at seven to Lord Howe out of the domestic terminal 3. The terminal serves only Qantas flights and has sixteen gates and many shops and restaurants. My Qantas plane had only window seats at its ten rows. I had a nice window seat in row 2, so I could get some nice photos on takeoff and landing. The island is 360 miles from the Australian coast, and the flight was two hours. The passengers and I were served a nice box breakfast.

Lord Howe Island has only 380 residents and up to 400 tourists a year. It is a small island shaped like a cone. Upon landing, I had a nice view of Bowels Pyramid, a nearby island. The small airport is near two beautiful mountains and is being renovated. Because of the renovation work, there were two large tents next to the terminal, one with a check-in booth and the other with chairs to wait in. There were two small planes parked near the terminal; one had an engine missing, and the other was banged up from a crash years ago.

A lady from Earls Anchorage Hotel was waiting for me in the hotel van. Other passengers were also being picked up by other hotel vans as there were no taxis. Jenny owned the hotel and told me as we started on the ride to town that it was going to be hard to see the island in only one and a half days. Just about that time, another van came in the opposite direction, and Jenny stopped her van and waved down the other driver. He was Peter Phillips, owner of Chase 'n' Thyme Island Tours, the only tour agency on the island. He told Jenny that he had a tour under way with eight passengers and that it was the only one he was doing on the weekend.

Jenny asked me if I would like to join Peter's group, and I agreed as it would have been my only chance to have a tour of the island. I was reminded that I have some wonderful guardian angels looking after me.

From near the airport, Peter resumed the tour with his detailed narrative about the areas we passed, the many wild birds we saw, and a lot about the history of the island as well as a few tales. Peter said that one species of bird flies north to Alaska when it gets cold on Lord Howe then flies back with chicks during the Australian summers. He had a remarkable memory for details of many things. Peter told us that he came to the island about seven years ago, met his wife Janine, and stayed. She was born on the island as were her parents, grandparents, and great-grandparents. They have two teenage daughters studying in Sydney. One must stay on the island ten years to qualify for residency. Before Peter came to the island, he had various jobs on the mainland and even worked in Aspen, Colorado, for a couple of years. I got to meet Janine as the group had tea, coffee, and cupcakes at her home about halfway through the tour. One story that Peter told was that about a dozen years ago, forty-seven tourists got very sick having steak butchered from the local cattle. The authorities had a difficult time getting all the tourists to the mainland as the runway is only a half a mile long and not long enough to land large planes. After this tragedy, the government banned all local beef and only allowed certified beef to be delivered from the mainland. I brought a lot of laughter from the group when I said, "So your local McDonalds' must get all its hamburger from Sydney." (There are only three restaurants on the island, and the Anchorage, owned by the hotel, is the biggest and most popular restaurant.)

On the tour, I only saw a few yield signs but no stop signs. Of course, there is only one main two-lane road, Lagoon Road, that goes only about halfway across the island. There are numerous other one-lane roads going to various homes. Peter said there are hiking trails up both mountains, but they are challenging most of the way; for example, Mt. Eliza is 450 feet, Kiai's Lookout 550 feet, and Malabar 870 feet above sea level. There are several nice sandy beaches and a cargo ship dock at the terminal. On the tour, I only saw a few cars but many more tourists on rented bikes. We also passed a cemetery, hospital, post office, two banks, museum, three churches, and three restaurants. Mt. Eliza is at the west end of the island, and the other two mountains are on the east side of the long island. Peter told the group that the island was once several small islands that were joined with sand deposits. There were also several different names given to the island. Since the island was small and there were no whales nearby, whalers only stopped at the island for fresh water. On the tour, we drove by a nineteen-hole golf course as well as bowling club. There is a small school, but all the high school students go to the mainland if they want to continue their education. Crime is nonexistent on the island, but there is a cop who also serves several other duties. We stopped at the waste recycling plant, where almost all the trash and organic waste are treated or recycled and used.

Following the tour, Peter dropped me off at the Anchorage restaurant, where I met Jenny again. She drove me up the road about half a mile to the Anchorage Hotel. She took me into an individual cottage called Tarpon 3 so I could drop my backpack off, and then we returned to the restaurant, where I had lunch. After my meal, I went across the street to Thompson's store that was next to the post office. There, I did a little shopping for a baseball hat, a magnet, and postcards. After returning to the restaurant, Jenny drove me back to the hotel.

My bungalow is a freestanding building, and there are about a dozen others on the hotel grounds that sit next to the ocean. The bungalow is very spacious with a large bedroom, living room, dining room, and kitchen. There is also a spacious bathroom with the biggest bathtub I have ever used as well as a nice deck with table and chairs. Out back is a big water tank, where rainwater is collected. It is filtered before it goes into the bungalow's water system. The wastewater is treated and used for toilet water. Later, I asked Jenny why the toilet water was yellow and did not taste good. She laughed. There were solar panels on the roof that supplied the electricity and a TV that had more than a hundred channels. There were no keys for the bungalow as it was always left unlocked because of the low incidence for crime.

On Sunday, I left Lord Howe Island at three and arrived in Sydney at five. I then went via train and bus to the Verin hotel in Randwick, my old neighborhood when I worked at the University of New South Wales for three years. I had dinner at Skandels restaurant nearby that is now an Italian restaurant named something else. My activities the next day consisted of a walk about Randwick and the university then into the city to walk around Circular Quay and the nearby Rocks. I ate at an Irish pub that was billed as the oldest Irish pub in Australia. There was a sign on the front door of the pub that read, "Please do not feed the birds." I got some laughter from the waitress as I said, "I guess you cannot feed me since I am an ex-jailbird."

On Tuesday, after checking out at the Verin Randwick, I took bus 372 to Central Station and then caught the train to the international terminal. This terminal is big and full of nice shops and restaurants. I went to gate 60 at one end of the airport, where the Air New Zealand lounge is located. I had some free food and drink there. The flight to Auckland boarded at eleven and was fully loaded. I was happy as I got put in luxurious business class to be pampered for three hours. The plane landed in Auckland at five, two hours behind Sydney time. Then I left Auckland at eight on a turbo jet Air New Zealand plane that held about forty passengers. The four-hour flight landed in Rarotonga Cook Island at one in the morning on the same day we left New Zealand. We had crossed the International Date Line. Upon arrival, all the passengers were met by a beautiful young lady. The young lady's greeting was "La Orana," which means "You live long." It is a unique first gesture of friendship from the special Polynesian people, renowned for their hospitality and warmth.

The Cook Islands are in 1.3 million square miles of the Pacific. All the islands combined make up a land area of just 140 square miles. Each island is unlike the other, and all have their own special features. From the majestic peaks of Rarotonga to the low-lying, untouched coral atolls of the northern islands of Manihiki, Penrhyn, Rakahanga, Pukapuka, Nassau, and Suwarrow. The latter island, inhabited only by a caretaker and his family, is a popular anchorage for yachts from all over the world. The Southern Cooks are made up of the capital, Rarotonga, and Aitutaki, Atiu, Mangaia, Mauke, Mitiaro, Manuae, Palmerston, and Takutea. Takutea is an uninhabited bird sanctuary and managed by the Atiu Island Council. Manuae is the remaining uninhabited island. Cook Islanders have their own Maori language and each of the populated islands a distinct dialect. It has a population of around thirteen thousand. The Cooks have been self-governing in free association with New Zealand since 1965. By virtue of that unique relationship, all Cook Islanders have New Zealand passports. The country is governed by a twenty-five-member Parliament elected by universal suffrage. The Cook Islands Parliamentary system is modeled on the Westminster system of Britain. The queen's representative is head of state. A House of Ariki (traditional paramount chiefs) counsels and advises government, as does the Koutu Nui, a body of traditional chiefs.

Rarotonga is the vibrant ear of the Cook Islands nation and the country's seat of government. The largest island, at forty square miles, Rarotonga is home to more than half of the country's population. The lush, mountainous interior of Rarotonga rises to two thousand feet, providing a dramatic backdrop to the coast, where most of the settlements can be found. Avarua is the island's commercial center. This lively township has all the main services and excellent shopping and dining. Rarotonga's beautiful lagoon is sheltered by the reef that circles the island. The lagoon offers a host of activities from windsurfing and sailing to glass-bottom boat tours, while the open sea beyond the reef has great game fishing and diving. Palm-fringed beaches of white sand add to the island's tropical beauty. All international flights to the Cooks arrive at Rarotonga Airport, which is two and a half miles from Avarua township.

A bus from the Edgewater Resort picked me and ten guests up at the airport and brought us to the hotel that is about three miles from the airport. I did not have a reservation for the morning, only one for Tuesday and Wednesday nights, so I had to pay an extra $75 to get into the room, twelve hours earlier than normal check-in. The room was nice, on the second level of a motel-type building, with a kitchen, bathroom (shower only), and large open bedroom with a double bed. I was happy to have a bed since I was tired. I slept in that morning but did manage to get to the dining room in another building just before they stopped serving breakfast at eleven. The dining room overlooks an outdoor dining area that is next to a nice swimming pool and a beautiful beach; the ocean waters are a beautiful green color. Next to the pool are two ping-pong tables. There is also a large tennis court nearby.

After breakfast, I had a walk about the hotel grounds that are quite large. The main road going around the island is about a block from the hotel. After my walk, I took a nap *then caught the public bus that picks up passengers in front of the hotel lobby. It circles the island every hour and only costs $5. I made a round trip without getting off the bus. The island is beautiful with tree-covered mountains in the middle and beautiful beaches paralleling the other side of the road. The bus went by many roadside restaurants and resorts, a few churches with small graveyards, and many nice homes, most in the tsunami danger zone. There were also several places to rent bikes, motorbikes, and cars and a few gas-food stations. I only saw one large food market. The bus made about two dozen stops as well as where people waved the bus down. After circling the island, I had a pasta dinner at the Spaghetti House next to the Edgewater Resort. During the day, there had been a few short rainstorms accompanied by scary loud thunder.*

The next day, the showers were even more intense and more often. After breakfast, I took the bus into Avarua's main shopping area, where the stores are next to one another on about a ten-block area. There is a small harbor for tour boats, many restaurants, souvenir shops, police station, bank, school, church, museum, University of South Pacific, cinema, post office, and supermarket. Avarua is on the north side of the island, and the airport is located about equidistant from the town and the Edgewater Resort. There is a walking path that runs out of Avarua across the south side of the island to Vaimaanga. There is a smaller shopping village called Muri that is located on the east side of the island. It appeared that almost all the islanders are Polynesian and mostly overweight. Lord Howe Island was just the opposite, almost all Australian Caucasians. I had dinner at the hotel restaurant next to the beach and swimming pool. It was a beautiful evening outside, and the hotel band played music. Following breakfast the next morning, a taxi picked me up for my one-hour Air New Zealand flight to Aitutaki Cook leaving at ten thirty.

At the Rarotonga Airport before departure, there was no one at the Air New Zealand check-in counters as well as the Jetstar and Virgin Australia Airlines desks, so I went over to the Air Rarotonga desk, and it was their airline that I would be flying to Aitutaki on. I got my boarding pass without showing any identification, and at the gate or upon boarding the aircraft, no one checked my passport. There was also no security check. The airport has only one domestic departure gate and another one for international travel. I boarded an Embraer Bandeirante plane that had only sixteen window seats. There were nine fellow passengers. Prior to takeoff, the copilot told us that we would be having some turbulence about halfway. There was no stewardess and no cockpit door. Indeed, we did have some scary bouncing around halfway with some rain showers. It reminded me of the flight to Kaieteur Falls in Guyana, where the small plane went through a terrible rainstorm with wild turbulence. After landing, a beautiful young lady greeted us at the terminal, then I got a nice-smelling lei from Eileen, who met me and another couple from Austria. She took us on about half-a-mile ride to the hotel in the hotel shuttle van. The Austrians were planning to spend a week on Aitutaki. They had also spent a week on Rarotonga to escape the cold weather in Europe. They were a nice-looking couple in their fifties, and I told them about my living there for three years and two summers.

Aitutaki is 130 miles north from Rarotonga and has one of the most magnificent lagoons in the world with small uninhabited islands on its surrounding reef; it is unquestionably the most picturesque of the Cooks southern group islands. It is protected by an outlying reef, and the island's lagoon size is seven by nine miles and home to many small motu. The lagoon boasts crystal clear turquoise waters and dazzling white sand beaches and is home to around two thousand people. Aitutaki is the Cook's second-most populated island, but the pace of life is noticeably slower than that of Rarotonga. Arutanga is on the west coast and is the main village with its collection of shops, post office, and a small wharf. A road circles Aitutaki, hugging the coast most of the way.

I stayed at the Aitutaki Village with its Blue Lagoon Restaurant on Ootu Beach. The hotel sits next to a white sandy beach with adjoining beautiful blue-green lagoon. There were sixteen separate bungalows, and I had number 4. It has a porch, large bedroom with small table, desk, and adjoining kitchen. The bathroom was separate. The whole inside was stained pine with an open ceiling. However, there was no television. I had arranged for a rental car, and it was dropped off at two. It was a black Mazda van that held eight passengers. I then drove around most of the roads on the island, taking lots of pictures until dinnertime at seven. I was amazed that I had no trouble driving on the left side of the road. At first, however, I kept turning on the wipers instead of the turn signal. There were only a few cars on the roads and many more motorbikes, scooters, and some tourist peddle bikes. On the trip, I counted lots of roaming chickens, six cats, nine goats, and two pigs. There are no dogs on Aitutaki, and no one is permitted to bring them onto the island. The island is covered in rainforests of palm and coconut trees, with a few houses scattered around. Most of the people live on the west side of the island, where there are a few stores on a dock, several grocery stores, gas stations, post office, bank, school, hospital, many resort lodges and villas for tourists, and six Christian churches. Only a few buildings and several abandoned buildings were on the central east side of the island as well as the southern tip. The island is long, and the airport and my hotel and a few others were on a narrow thumb of the island, along with a golf course.

There are fourteen much smaller islands around the Aitutaki Lagoon and a paved two-lane road on the west side of the island that is connected with a gravel two-lane road on the east side. The lower part of the island has six two-lane roads connecting the west and east side roads. The road on the south end of the island is one lane and dirt as was part of the roads going to the two high parts of the island. I drove both roads and was worried in a few places that I might get stuck in the mud. The road to the Piraki Lookout, where there are two water tanks, was nice going up the west side but divided on the other side into two narrow dirt roads. At the fork in the road, I took a right-hand turn to find out the road turned into a grass path that led to a small home on a hill with great views. Of course, I then turned around and went back to the place where the other two roads met and took the left-hand road from the lookout. That dirt road was narrow and curvy and eventually met the two-lane west road. It was quite a four-hour driving adventure. Without the car, I would have been stuck at Aitutaki Village since there were no tours that afternoon. In fact, there was only one land tour, called a safari tour, that only went around the island.

After dinner on Friday night, there were several severe rainstorms that had scary thunder. However, the next morning was beautiful, and I enjoyed the view of the lagoon as I was eating a delicious buffet breakfast. Only the Austrian couple was at the outdoor restaurant with me. After breakfast, I took a couple of extra slices of bread and was having fun feeding several chickens and their chicks next to the deck. Of course, several birds came down for breakfast, but the chickens ate everything.

There was a lagoon tour, but it did not sound that exciting to me, and besides that, I had the car until two. After breakfast, I retraced yesterday's trip but did go on several small roads that I did not see yesterday. After I refilled the gas tank and returned the car, the same young man who brought the car yesterday drove me back to the village. He had grown up on the island and was attending the University of Auckland to become an architectural engineer. Of course, he was now on summer break. I asked him who owned the chickens on the island, and the young man told me, "No one. Once a year, people go out and capture a few for meals."

It was sunny most of the day except for a short light rain shower that I got caught in on a short walk. At the hotel, I had a light lunch, napped, and got caught up on my diary writing until dinner at six. After dinner, I watched a beautiful sunset. My bungalow was nice since I could make all the noise I wanted and did not have to be irritated by neighbors' noise as in a hotel room. The bungalow at Lord Howe had the same good feature.

Following breakfast on Saturday morning, Eileen took me to the airport for my one-hour flight to Rarotonga. The plane was a SAAB 340 with fifteen rows of window seats on the plane's left side and aisle and window seats on the right side. We had a stewardess that served drinks. Before takeoff, I spoke with a British couple. The guy was a mechanical engineer, so naturally, I told them my mechanical engineer joke. They got a kick out of it and said they plan to tell their daughter. Upon landing in Rarotonga, I was reminded how beautiful the mountains are as well as the large beautiful lagoon.

It had been raining off and on, but we managed to leave Rarotonga in a fully loaded Airbus 320R with three seats on both sides of the aisle. When we landed in Auckland, after the four-hour flight, the rain was much worse than in the Cook Islands. We had crossed the International Date Line, so we had lost a day.

At the airport, I managed to catch the Jet Park Hotel shuttle bus after a five-minute wait. The bus ran every *thirty minutes. The hotel was nice, and I had green pea soup for dinner. That night, I had trouble sleeping and was still awake at two. Early the next morning, I took the shuttle to the airport. The Air New Zealand flight was five hours, arriving in Papeete at four. We had gained a day. The Papeete airport is small with only three domestic gates. During my wait at immigration, I met a couple from Pittsburgh. They were on their honeymoon and planned to go to Bora Bora after a few days in Tahiti. He is a medical doctor, and she is a pharmacist. At the airport, I exchanged $100 for 750 Republic of Frances.*

The Air Tahiti plane left Papeete at six fully loaded with two-by-two seats and twenty-five rows. After the plane's arrival in Raiatea at seven, Geovanti, my taxi driver, met me at the gate holding a sign with the hotel name, Buddha Villa, and my name. An elderly lady came, and after her luggage arrived, Giovanti dropped her in town and me at the Villa. Charlotte, a lovely young lady, was waiting in the driveway of her home. I was surprised that I would be staying in a house doing hotel business. The home was nice, however, with three guest rooms and a bedroom for Charlotte and her boyfriend, Yoann, a young Frenchman who owned a small construction company. Of course, the home had a nice big kitchen and living and dining rooms. Everyone had to share one bathroom (shower) and a separate toilet. There were two nice covered decks. The home has a small grassy yard in front and back and sits on the side of a hill. It is surrounded by mountains and jungle on three sides. The home is quiet except for a few roosters crowing, and every once in a while, one can hear a car go by but not seen. I am the only guest.

The home belongs to Charlotte's mother, who is now living in the Caribbean with her boyfriend, who had gotten transferred there by his employer. She is British as is Charlotte. But of course, Charlotte had learned French. The mother had left behind a big dog, Beckie, and two gray cats, Takia and Fabada (meaning "fat one"). Charlotte's mom is a Buddhist, so there are several Buddhist statues in the home, and a big one outside. Charlotte has a sister in England.

On Monday morning, I was up at seven as Charlotte had a light breakfast waiting for me. It was still raining off and on, and during the night, there were several serious episodes of torrential rain that woke me up. Charlotte told me the weather is bad because we were on the edge of a cyclone that was now centered around the Cook Islands. It came in the day after I left the Cooks. I really liked staying here as it reminded me of staying at Bret and Elda's homes several times in Port Elizabeth and in Stilbaai. Later, as I was sitting on the sofa on the patio next to the kitchen while waiting on the rental car to be delivered, one of the cats jumped up next to me, then jumped up behind me on the back of the couch, then went through the open kitchen window to the countertop. It was something Cochise, Lorrie's exploration cat, would do. A young man from the car rental company arrived and took me to town to sign car rental papers. I had rented a small Fiat that was much easier to drive than the car in Aitutaki since driving was on the right side of the road here.

According to Polynesian legends, Raiatea is known as "Havai," the sacred, and the Marae of Taputapuatea was the political, cultural, and religious center of the "Maohi civilization." Raiatea has a population of about twelve thousand and is about 160 miles north of Tahiti; it is the capital of the Leeward Islands. The town center of Utura is about a fifteen-minute walk from the villa, past a large high school. The town has two post offices, police station, marina, hospital, pharmacy, two large grocery stores, many other shops, and a few restaurants. There is also a small family hotel and three banks. The main road of 60 miles goes around the island, and there is another road that crosses the island between Faaroa and Futuna, two small villages. At the top of the crossover road is Belvedere, a lookout with great views over Faaroa Bay, the summit of the volcano, Oropiro, Nao Nao Motu, and a vast jungle of rainforest with lots of coconut and palm trees. The mountains and hills on the island are beautiful. Temehani mountain is the only place in the world where the rare and protected gardenia flower, "Tiare Apetahi," grows. There is also the magnificent Sugarloaf of Fareatai with a beautiful waterfall as well as many other narrow and high waterfalls on several other mountains.

I got to observe these island features on a drive around the island. It was cloudy with light rain and sometimes very heavy rain that looked like sea waves coming down the road pushed by a strong wind. First, I drove the car into town, parked it, and had a walk in the shopping area of town next to the pier. The shopping area is on both sides of three blocks of the town and on another parallel street as well. I did find a baseball hat for my hat collection. I then started my drive around the island. There were few cars on the road that mostly paralleled the ocean. Occasionally, there were clusters of homes and, of course, many around the town. I liked the island more than Aitutaki because of its spectacular and beautiful mountains. Of course, Aitutaki has the beautiful blue-green lagoon.

The town of Otutoa sits on the narrow north end of the island, and five minutes after I left, I went by the small airport, then Sunset Beach where there were a few surfers. At the six-mile mark on the west side of the island, there was the Chambres d'hôtes Temehani. Next, I went through the small village of Tevaitoa, then another village, Tehuru, that is near Mt. Toomaru at three thousand feet and about twelve miles from Uturoa. Between Tevaitoa and Tehuru is Maraejeinuu and Anapa Perle Shop, a beautiful blue building on the beach selling pearls. About fifteen miles from town is another small village, Vaiaau, then Fetuuce at twenty-five miles, and Puohine at the thirty-mile marker. This is the south end of the island that is about twice the width as the north end. Between these two small villages is the road that crosses the island to the village of Faaroa. I drove across the island on that road then came back to resume my travels with the ocean on my right side. I was almost to Opoa when I stopped at the Hotel Opoa Beach for a lunch of pizza. After I left the hotel and continued my ride on the east side of the island, I had to turn around as a tree had blown over and blocked the road. At first, I waited a while to see if anyone would come and perhaps assist me in moving the tree, but no one came along. I then retraced my route and went over the road that crossed the island and continued my drive from Opoa back to Uturoa. Between the hotel and Upoa was Marge de Taputapuatea. Periodically along the route were covered waiting booths for the bus. I also passed a big fenced-in cattle ranch that was next to the ocean. At this point, the heavy rain started again, and I was forced to pull over since I could not see the road. The small villages I went through on the final part of the trip were Faaroa and Avera. I had another walk about Uturoa before returning the car. By the way, there is another large island of Taha'a that is near the north end of the island and Uturoa.

That evening, I ate some of the things I had bought at the supermarket. I had my meal on the patio adjoining my room, and the dog joined me. I shared some of my sardines and potato chips with him. Later, I checked my e-mail on Charlotte's computer and made an early night of it. Following a small breakfast the next morning, I did some writing, took a nap, and watched the rain come and go from the covered patio. Charlotte fixed a nice lunch, and about five, Giovani took me to the two-gate airport for my Air Tahiti flight at seven back to Tahiti. However, I had to wait an extra hour since they had to change planes because of *mechanical problems. The plane also had a short stop at the nearby island of Huahine. At eleven, I boarded my Air Tahiti flight to Los Angeles. On the flight, I had the aisle seat, and Katie was sitting at the window. She is young and beautiful, lives in Chicago, and plays the piano on a cruise ship. She has a bachelor's degree in music and was very pleasant to talk with. After the plane arrived in Los Angeles at nine on Valentine's Day, I went through immigration and customs, then caught a Delta Air Lines flight to Denver at two and arrived at five in the evening. It had been a wonderful trip full of adventure.*

Following the long transatlantic flight and plane changes in Munich and Stockholm, John and Lara arrive safely in Gothenburg, but tired. The Gothenburg airport is nice and new with ten gates. After John exchanged $200 for 1,500 kronor, they took a taxi to the hotel for 550 kronor. Everything in Sweden is expensive.

Gothenburg is a beautiful city surrounded by hills on one side and the Mediterranean Sea on the other side. It has a population of one million. During John and Lara's three nights in Gothenburg, they stayed at the Radisson Blu Riverside Got, a nice hotel and only four months old. Their room was on the tenth floor of the twelve-story building with great views of part of the city. After unpacking, they walked across the street, where the International Solvent Extraction Conference was being held. The building is large with offices on the upper floors and the conference center and several restaurants on the bottom floor. Next door is Chalmers University, where John had given lectures in the past. A couple of blocks toward the river is a dock for the free ferry that takes mainly students across the Gota river to the older part of the city.

When they arrived in the conference center, they found out that the conference reception was already under way. The couple was met by the conference organizer, Professor Christian.

for a trip to each end of the city and into parts of the suburbs. There are many high-rise apartment buildings but only a few single-family homes. In the city, there are many pedestrian-only streets. They had an early dinner at McDonald's. There are at least three other McDonald's in the city as well as a Burger King, KFC, and several Subways. It looked like there were 7-Elevens at every street corner.

The couple had to wake at four on Wednesday morning, August 30, for a taxi ride in the rain to the airport for their KLM flight to Amsterdam at six. In Amsterdam, they got a flight to Newcastle, UK, that took one and a half hours and then an hour flight on Eastern Airways to the Isle of Man. They only had fifteen minutes between both connections. They arrived on the Isle of Man at ten thirty and went by taxi to the Palace Hotel and Casino in the main city of Douglas for a two-night stay; it was raining there just like in Amsterdam and Newcastle. Their taxi driver was from Transylvania in Romania and had been in Douglas for five years. His girlfriend was from Slovakia. They had a four-month-old daughter. He told the couple that the Isle of Man is a tax haven, and unemployment is only 1 percent. He also told them that since August 24, there had been the world-renowned motorcycle races around the island that were founded in 1908. They were to race again on Sunday for the Traveler Trophy. The bikers were mainly from the UK. They had brought their bikes over on the ferry with most of them there to only watch the races. As they were traveling near their hotel, they saw many motorcycles parked outside hotels, and the outdoor restaurants were full of bikers drinking and eating. The races continued until September 3.

The hotel is quite old, and the adjoining casino is the only one on the island. The city is the largest town on the island, the Borough of Douglas, and it has a McDonald's, Pizza Hut, and two Dominos; however, the couple ate at the hotel restaurant and had fish both nights. During lunch, John commented to Lara, "I have a hard time understanding most of the Brits. Do you?"

"As you know, I have a slight British accent since I perfected my English at Oxford and, of course, have no trouble understanding them."

"I even had a hard time at Clemson University understanding some of the people who grew up there and spoke with a Southern drawl. Of course, I also had trouble understanding a lot of the Australians when I worked there for three years."

Following lunch, they caught the number 1 two-decker bus that took them through town and the suburbs, past a few other small communities, and to the airport. A few miles past the airport is a small town called Castletown. It has the big and beautiful Rushen Castle located in the middle of the town. The couple took some pictures from the top floor of the bus. Then the bus continued west into Port Erin and then turned around and retraced the route back to Douglas. A steam train goes on the same route, but they did not have the time to take it.

In town, they took a walk on the curved boardwalk next to the large bay. Their hotel is on one end of the walk, near the start of the electric train and the end stop of the horse-drawn tram that rides on rails. The horse-drawn tram starts at the other end of the bay, about one mile away, and was built in 1876. The couple then walked over to the pedestrian walking street, where there were many shops selling everything, including lots of T-shirts and hats signifying the bike races. John commented that many cars had license plates with JJC, followed by three numbers.

The next morning, it was rainy and cold, but John and Lara had borrowed umbrellas from the hotel and walked back into the shopping district so John could check his e-mail at the library. Next, they caught the horse-drawn tram and went to the other end to catch the electric train to Laxey. After arriving in Laxey, they had a walkabout and a look at the Great Laxey Wheel—the world's largest waterwheel. It was used in the past in the mining industry. They were lucky that it had stopped raining on their arrival, and the skies cleared.

After their half-hour Laxey visit, they caught the Snaefell Mountain electric train to the top of the highest mountain on the island, two thousand feet above sea level. On the thirty-minute ride, the couple saw three rabbits and lots of sheep and horses. There was a twenty-minute stop at the summit station with a wonderful view of a beautiful reservoir surrounded by grass-covered hills. One could see the seven kingdoms of England: Scotland, Wales, Ireland, and the Kingdoms of Mann, Celtic, and Norse Iegunites. On the way back down the mountain, the engineer and conductor had to work the mechanical brakes on both cars to keep the train from speeding down the mountain. Once the train reached the bottom, the couple got on another electric train and continued north to Ramsey, the end point. In Ramsey, they stayed on the tram, taking more pictures, and returned to Douglas. The route was eighteen miles along the coast, over gorse-topped hills and Victorian glens. Back at the hotel, Lara tried her luck in the casino. The hotel had given her a five-pound coupon for a free spin at the wheel. She lost the coupon on the first spin.

John and Lara went to their room after dinner for an early night's sleep since they had another early flight the next morning, Friday, September 1. They left the hotel by taxi at four thirty. Their driver was interesting. Julie was the owner of Julie's Taxis and told the couple that she was fifty-two. She tried to guess John's age as fifty. She owned three taxies, was married with boys fifteen and twenty-six, and had a large home on the other side of the island. They got to the airport in fifteen minutes and only saw three other cars on the road. The couple had a short wait outside the five-gate airport terminal since it did not open until five. John always liked to be early at the airport, and this time they had a two-hour wait before takeoff. They had breakfast at the only restaurant in the airport and looked around in a gift shop during their wait for their plane to Heathrow. After landing, they had to go through customs, immigration, and security, which almost caused them to miss their flight to Milan.

They arrived in Lampedusa from Milan midafternoon and were greeted by a driver with reserved car from the Puesta De Sol Residence House. The airport is close to the center of the small town, and the couple could hear planes taking off and landing from their residence. The hotel is in front of a bay full of docked boats, and their shared room is large with kitchen, two beds, and adjoining bath. John was disappointed that there was no bathtub as they had at the Isle of Man. That evening, they ate at a nearby restaurant at the suggestion of the young lady at the front desk. She had an assistant, but neither one could speak much English.

The front desk lady had arranged a boat trip for John and Lara to take after breakfast. She said it was about all there was to do on the island. The lady told them that the shoreline of the small island has seven beautiful Caldor coves and two grottos where a boat could go into. Nearby under water is a Madonnina or statue that can be seen only with scuba gear on. The waters near the shores are a beautiful green, and the Cala Guitgia has one of the most beautiful beaches in the world. She said the interior of the island is much like the desert in North Africa. The island is only seventy miles from Tunisia, has a population of about six thousand, and its main industries are fishing, agriculture, and tourism. Since the early 2000s, the island has become a primary European entry point for migrants from Africa.

The next morning after breakfast, the boat owner/captain, who could not speak English, arrived at the hotel and took the couple to a nearby boat for a day of cruising around the island.

When they got to the small fishing boat that had a pilothouse and small second deck, and two couples sunning themselves on the top deck, they met the captain's wife and daughter. John was very reluctant at this point to board since the small boat did not look seaworthy. After they boarded and left the bay, the boat entered the angry sea and started to be tossed about. At that point, John somehow managed to communicate to the captain, using mostly sign language, with one hand on his stomach and the other hand pointing to the shore. The captain understood and kindly got the couple back on solid ground. They then had a short walk to the hotel to take a nap. Later, they had a long walk and discovered nice pedestrian streets with various restaurants and shops. They had pizza for lunch at one of the Italian restaurants. Next, they found a shop where Lara bought a magnet and postcards. There were lots of people walking about, shopping, and eating. After their long walks in the shopping areas and by the beautiful coast, they had dinner, followed by returning to the hotel to watch a little TV before retiring for the night.

The couple slept in since their flight to Rome did not leave until midday. In Rome, they flew nonstop to St. Petersburg.

Chapter 5
Russian Adventures

I

On their flight to St. Petersburg, John tells Lara about his first visit to Russia with Margrit. "I had been taking pictures from the plane. When the stewardess spotted me, she announced that no pictures were to be taken. Margrit laughed. The damage had already been done. We discovered later that the photos were not out of the ordinary. When we arrived at the Leningrad airport, we were full of suspicions about Russia and really expected a lot of trouble with customs and so on. We filled out the customs form declaring what money and valuables we had. Margrit listed her wedding band as her only valuable. We then proceeded through immigration with only our passports being stamped and then to customs. The customs officer was very Western in speech and manner. He appeared apologetic to have to ask us any questions and said he was sorry to have to confiscate Margrit's book, *The Russians*, that she was carrying. He did not check our luggage, just took our word for what we had, and ushered us on through. This only took at the most five minutes.

"We then went into the arrival hall and found the Intourist booth. We were informed that our reservations were in order, that we would be staying at the Leningrad Hotel, and the hotel's driver would take us there. On the ride, we discovered that Leningrad must be one of the most beautiful cities in the world. We loved the wide tree-lined streets, the parks, statues, and the beauty of the city. Our driver pointed out some of the sights to us on the way to the hotel and was most courteous and helped us with our luggage into the hotel. The hotel was immense, and we got a nice room. We found a lot of things to muse but nothing to destroy our good time or to distract from what we were discovering. We found out that some of the Russian customs were strange to us such as service, which was very poor since the Russian workers seemed more interested in avoiding their job rather than seeing to it that we were accorded every courtesy. We practically had to tackle the waiter to have him wait on us. But we enjoyed the delicious food once it arrived."

"John, that was before the wall came down. As you know, the people have changed a lot since those dark days."

"After dinner at the Leningrad Hotel the first night, we went for a walk by the bridge that crosses the Neva River. There, we met three young Russian couples, and they invited us to join their party. We visited with them while they were drinking champagne. They offered us some, but Margrit told them in the little Russian she knew that we did not drink. I was amazed at how much her little knowledge of the Russian language helped us. We were enjoying the company of the young couples. We did not understand, however, what they told us. One young man stated that at midnight, the bridges would go up. Margrit and I briefly talked together and decided they were a terrorist group about to blow up the bridge. Further conversations revealed that the bridge would indeed go up at midnight, but that was to let the ships pass."

Lara chuckles. "Margrit sure sounds like a wonderful and fun to be with lady."

"Yes, she gave me more than twenty-five years of marvelous memories."

"I hope I can do the same for you, John."

"Before we left the riverbank, they gave us several handfuls of Russian candy and said it was for our children. We gave them all the gum that we had with us. Then we went back to the hotel and went to our room to see the beautiful moon radiating on the ripples of the Neva River.

"On Sunday morning, we took the city tour and, in the afternoon, toured Pavlovsk and the Hermitage. We had a delightful Intourist guide, and we enjoyed her as much as the Hermitage. I had several photos taken with my camera of the three of us before we parted. We had dinner at the hotel before being transported to the train station. We loved the Russian food, the 'follies' show at the hotel, and the way the Russians sang together. It was a beautiful experience."

"I think we will be seeing the same things in the next two days, although there are many changes in the city besides a name change and a large increase in population. I have heard that the traffic is especially bad."

"Margrit and I got some sleep on the Red Arrow Express to Moscow that left at midnight and arrived early morning. At the Moscow station, we were greeted by my friend Misa and his wife, Sonya. We were treated to the absolute best while in Moscow and were not allowed to spend any money except for our hotel room and anything we bought or ate out of their presence. We had three lavish parties thrown for us, two at Misa and Sonya's flat and the other at the International Hotel complete with a stage show, circus acts, dancing girls, gymnasts, and later a band playing both Russian and English music. The party was hosted by Misa, Oleg, and Dmitri and their wives, and the dinner was simply superb. We had plenty to eat and drink, and we danced and danced. We returned to our hotel via the subway, which I had read was the best subway system in the world. We were extremely impressed.

"We also attended the Russian Circus, where we sat in the first row, wishing we had our children with us. We were entertained by the famous Popov the clown. The Friday night before we left, Misa and Sonya had a dinner party for us at their apartment. We again had a bounty of food and drinks, which Sonya had spent the entire day preparing. We danced to American music and just had a ball. We honestly had a fantastic time in Moscow. I am sure this visit will be much better since I am traveling with you, my dear lovely friend. I hope to call you my wife soon after I have assurances that Andrei's brother is no longer a threat to kill me so that you do not come into harm's way."

"It would be wonderful and romantic if we left Russia as man and wife."

During the next two days in St. Petersburg, the couple took an organized tour to visit the usual tourist places and spent a lot of time at the Hermitage. On their early morning train ride to Moscow, they shared a cabin.

Lara's parents and her brother, Vadim, greeted the couple at the Moscow station. After loving hugs with her parents and brother, Lara introduced John. After the wonderful welcome, the five went to the Mikhailov's flat in Vadim's car. The two-bedroom flat is on the second floor of an apartment building a block away from the Mendeleev campus. John helped Vadim carry the luggage into Lara's two-bed room that John would be sharing with her.

After unpacking, they joined Lara's parents and Vadim in the living room, where John told the Mikhailovs a little about himself in a mixture of English and Russian. Lara's parents and brother could understand most of what John said, and they told him that they could understand written English completely. The conversation continued over a late lunch with mostly Lara telling her parents about her sabbatical in the United States and their trip.

Following their meal, Vadim offered to take John for a drive around Moscow. Before they departed, John said, "Thank you for a delicious lunch. Lara, you sure have wonderful parents and brother. I look forward to spending the next few days with you all and enjoying your wonderful hospitality."

On the tour, John discovered that Vadim's English was easy to understand. Later on the drive, Vadim commented, "Lara told me a lot about your traveling around the world and that you have visited every country except for Somalia and Yemen. What were your best three trips?"

"My number 1 trip was a second visit to Antarctica that included going over the Antarctic Circle. The first time I took the trip, it included visits to the Falkland, South Georgia, South Orkney, and South Sandwich Islands. My second-best adventure was visiting Greenland and the High Arctic. My travels on the train from Vladivostok to Moscow was number 3. On that trip, I had a chance to visit Lake Baikal. I got my bug for traveling when I was about ten. I had an uncle who worked on a merchant ship and traveled the seven seas. During the summers when he would return to Denver, he always gave us an interesting slideshow of his travels the past nine months. Where have you traveled to, Vadim?"

"Well, since I do not make a lot of money as a high school chemistry teacher, even though I do not have a wife and children to support, I have only been to a few cities in Western Russia and Eastern Europe."

"I assume your parents had an impact on your interest in chemistry."

"You are correct. Now we should head back to my folks for dinner."

After the three-hour drive, John gave his thanks to Vadim for showing him some places that he had not seen on previous trips to the city.

After a wonderful dinner, John excused himself for an early night's sleep. The foursome continued their conversations that started at dinner, and about an hour later, Vadim returned to his flat on the other side of Moscow. After Lara's parents retired, she got the volume of John's diary that he had brought on the trip and read about another one of his adventures. This one was his trip to Myanmar (Burma).

I flew out of Greenville-Spartanburg airport on Wednesday morning, November 28, at nine on a Delta Air Lines flight to Bangkok. I had plane changes in Detroit and Tokyo. The Detroit airport is big and modern. The last time

I was at the airport was following a trip to the High Arctic. It was during the time of a massive electrical outage in the northeast U.S., caused by a computer problem, and the Detroit airport had no power except for emergency generators. Even drinking water from the drinking fountains was not advised.

In Detroit, I had an hour layover prior to catching my Delta flight to Tokyo. The flight from Detroit to Tokyo was in a Boeing 747, and I had an aisle seat with the two middle seats vacant (two rows from the back). I watched three movies. The best one was Being Flynn *with Robert De Niro. De Niro played an aspiring writer who was an absent father as his son was growing up. His son also became an aspiring writer, and they both ended up in a homeless shelter together, the father an alcoholic and the son a drug user. A great movie!*

The other good movie was Australia. *I only watched half of the third movie,* Crocodile Dundee, *since I had seen it before. We had a two-hour layover in Tokyo and arrived in Bangkok the next day.*

On the last flight, I sat next to a guy (balding, sixty years old) from Michigan who was on his way to spend the winter (three months) with his Thai girlfriend. He had met her six years ago when she gave him a therapeutic massage. They correspond via e-mail the other times of the year. He told me that she is about thirty years old and beautiful. He gives her some money to support her parents. He says everything is very inexpensive in Thailand. The guy had several jobs, one was collecting antiques and buried valuables at old farms and selling them on eBay.

After arriving in Bangkok, I exchanged $180 for 2,332 baht then took a taxi to the Great Residence Hotel, about a ten-minute ride from airport (fare 50 baht). The hotel was $24 a night! I had arrived at one on Friday morning, and after checking in, the bellboy asked me if I wanted him to *send up a masseuse. I told him I was too tired. The room had two single beds, TV, refrigerator, and small bathroom. About midmorning, I took a taxi back to the airport, had breakfast, took a walk in the new and large airport, and got a one-hour foot and back massage for 600 baht. I caught my Thai Airways flight from Bangkok to Yangon at 1:00 p.m. (one-hour flight). On the plane, I was served a box lunch.*

Myanmar is bordered by India, Bangladesh, China, Laos, and Thailand. One-third of Myanmar's total perimeter forms an uninterrupted coastline along the Bay of Bengal and the Andaman Sea, and it is the fortieth largest country in the world and the second largest country in Southeast Asia. Myanmar is also the twenty-fourth most populous country in the world with over sixty million people. Naypyidaw is the nation's capital, with Yangon being the largest city. Burmese is the official language. Since independence from Great Britain in 1948, the country has been in one of the longest-running civil wars among the country's myriad ethnic groups that remain unresolved. From 1962 to 2011, the country was under military rule. The military junta was officially dissolved in 2011, following a general election in 2010 and a nominally civilian government installed, though the military retains enormous influence. Myanmar is a resource-rich country. However, the Myanmar economy is one of the least developed in the world, and the health care system is one of the worst.

In Myanmar, the driving from the left side to the right side of the road began in 1947. I thought it must be difficult driving since the steering wheels in most of the cars are on the right side. Of course, if you are an American mailman, then it is no problem.

Yangon, previously named Rangoon, is a modern city of five million people with a history of over two millennia. It was rebuilt on a grid plan in the 1850s, and the wide tree-lined boulevards are bordered by fine stone buildings. In the

1880s, Yangon was renowned as the Queen of the East. The center of the city has older apartment buildings mixed with new ones and small shops selling everything from antique lacquer ware to silver-backed dress table sets left over from colonial days.

Several weeks prior to my visit, a 6.8 magnitude quake hit Central Myanmar and killed as many as twelve people, collapsed a bridge, damaged ancient Buddhist pagodas, and caved in several mines. Mandalay is located about seventy miles south of the epicenter near the town of Shwebo, and the smaller towns in the area, that is a center for the mining of minerals and gemstones, were hit the worst.

My Myanmar visit was from November 30 to December 6. Richard Myat Tun Win met me at the Yangon airport, and his driver drove me to the Strand Hotel, arriving about three. The Strand is a five-star hotel across the street from a shopping area and a few blocks from the center of the city. The Strand was originally built in 1901 by John Darwood, and then it was acquired by the legendary Sarkies Brothers (of Raffles fame) as one of the Southeast Asia's grand colonial hotels. From the beginning, the Strand was regarded as "the finest hostelry east of Suez" and Murray's A Handbook for Travellers in India, Burma and Ceylon, *1911 edition, stated that the hotel was patronized by "royalty, nobility, and distinguished personages." I was now on the guest register with George Orwell, Sir Peter Ustinov, Somerset Maugham, David Rockefeller, Sir Noel Coward, Rudyard Kipling, and HRH King Taufa'ahau Tupou IV of Tonga (in 1936).*

That afternoon, Richard took me on a walk near the hotel. We strolled around colonial monuments, port tower, inland water transport, supreme court, telegraph office, Baptist church, clock tower, independence monument, Sule Pagoda, and city hall until about four.

From 5:00 to 6:30 p.m., we visited the Shwedagon Pagoda. This architectural masterpiece is a golden fantasy of gilded stupas, serene Buddhas, and mythical beasts said to be 2,500 years old. According to legend, eight hairs of the last Buddha are enshrined within the pagoda. The outside of the stupa is plated with 8,688 solid gold sabs, and the tip of the stupa is set with 5,448 diamonds and 2,317 rubies, sapphires, and topaz. A huge emerald sits in the middle to catch the first and last rays of the sun. It had just rained, and the marble floors were very slippery; I had to hang on to Richard to keep from falling. A little later, the president of Vietnam came through with an entourage of guards and accompanying delegates from both countries. A week earlier, Pres. Barack Obama had visited the city, the first U.S. president to do so.

That night, I skipped dinner and had a ninety-minute massage in my room. The masseuse was young and brought her own massage table. After she left, I took a long hot bath in a big tub.

After a good breakfast the next morning (December 1), I joined Richard for a whole day of activities that included seeing the railway station, minister's office, St. Paul Catholic church, Botataung market, and a look at the Rangoon River. We also visited the Botataung Paya (Pagoda), a 131-foot stupa that is hollow, allowing visitors to be able to walk around inside it. The original pagoda was destroyed in 1943 when it took a direct hit from an Allied bomb. After the bombing, a golden casket containing a hair and two other relics of Buddha was found.

Later that morning, we visited the reclining Buddha pagoda, which is not a pagoda but a pavilion housing a 230-foot statue. Within the pagoda enclosure is a center devoted to the study of sacred Buddhist manuscripts. About six hundred monks live in the monastery and spend their days studying and meditating. We got to observe them having lunch, their last meal of the day. Most of the monks

During all the places I visited (except when the Vietnam president came through the pagoda that Obama and Clinton had also visited), I only saw a few soldiers and police. As was typical of other countries, the people were nice and the children beautiful. I had always envisioned Myanmar as a jungle, but what I saw was mostly flat farmland with some hills and mountains.

Our flight to Bangkok was short (about an hour), arriving approximately at two. I had to wait until midnight for my flight to Brisbane. Since I have United Gold Medallion status, I got into the Thai Airways lounge and had some free food, Internet use, and rest. I also got a forty-five-minute foot massage.

II

Following breakfast on their second day in Moscow, Lara takes John to Mendeleev University to show him around campus and her office. She also introduces him to a few of her colleagues and the head of the department. She tells her boss about her activities during the last six months in Colorado. After spending the morning at the university, they return to the apartment.

After lunch, Misa meets John at the Mikhailov's apartment. Misa's driver, Alexander, then drives John and Misa to Misa's academy office for some technical discussions. Later, they go to the academy's high-rise building for coffee at the top floor cafe. Following their break, Misa offers John a chance to go to the building's roof for some picture taking. Misa tells John, "Only workmen have been allowed to take the stairs to the roof where they are constructing an observation deck. Since they are not working today, would you like to have a visit there since you can get pictures of the city in all directions?"

"Certainly. I never miss an opportunity to get the best shots."

After climbing the stairs and arriving at the deck, Misa warns John, "Be careful since the deck is still under construction, and the hand railings have not been installed yet."

"Thanks, Misa. You were right about this being a great place to take some spectacular pictures of the city."

"I did not think the view of the city would be so great. Please excuse me since I would like to briefly return to my office to get my camera. I should be back in about ten minutes."

After John finishes his picture taking near the edge of the platform opposite the stairway, a man quietly enters the platform and runs at John with the intention of pushing him over the ledge. However, John sees the man out of the corner of his eye and jumps out of his way. The man then falls off the platform to the street below. A very shaken John goes down the stairs and elevator to the street, where he meets Misa. John tells Misa what happened and says, "I think this guy is Andrei's brother, and he tried to kill me, thinking I killed his brother and two nephews."

Misa advises John not to say anything to the police and that he will do all the talking. "I plan to tell the police we do not know the man or why he jumped."

They then walk over to join several other people near the body. One person says, "This man is dead. Can someone please call the police?"

Ten minutes later, a police car and ambulance arrive. Next, another police car arrives with the police captain. He searches the dead man's pockets and pulls out his wallet. After finding his driver's license, the captain asks the small crowd, "This man is Alexei Pushkin. Does anyone know him?"

No one answers the captain, but a few minutes later, Misa speaks up. "I do not know the man, but I saw him jump from the top of the Academy of Sciences high-rise. I work in the adjoining building. I assume he committed suicide."

The captain agrees, and as he is dispersing the growing crowd, the ambulance crew takes Pushkin to the morgue. Misa and John, still unnerved, return to the academy office. Misa makes a call to Alexander and asks him to take John back to the Mikhailov's apartment.

After John arrives back at the apartment, still shaken up, he asks Lara to come to the bedroom to talk. He tells her about what happened at the academy, and she starts crying. "Oh, John, I am so sorry this frightening thing has happened to you. What can I do to help you?"

"Thank you, Lara, but I will be okay, but it might take a few days to recover from this ordeal. The only good thing about Pushkin's death is that I do not have to worry about him trying to kill me. Now we can get married!"

Over dinner, Lara tells her parents that she and John want to get married on Friday morning, the day before they leave Moscow. "We agreed not to have a traditional church ceremony for their wedding, only the required civil ceremony in the department of public services. Following the fifteen-minute ceremony with the exchanging of rings, we would like to return here for the wedding party if you agree. We would also like you both to witness the civil ceremony as required by law."

Lara's parents jump from the table and congratulate the two with hugs and kisses. Lara's mom says, "Of course, we will stand up for you both and host the party. Now we need to start making an attendee list and make a few phone calls."

John and Lara spend the next two days getting ready for the party as well as applying for the civil ceremony. Everything went according to their plans, and all the invitees can attend the party on Friday night.

Following the Friday morning ceremony and returning to the Mikhailov's apartment, Lara's father gives crystal glasses to both the bride and groom and are asked to proceed with the tradition of breaking the glasses. He tells John, "The number of broken pieces is supposed to indicate the number of years you will spend happily together." John drops his glass on the marble floor, breaking it into many pieces. The surprised group witnesses Lara's glass not breaking after she drops it on the marble floor.

Later in the afternoon, the guests start arriving. Of course, Lara's brother is the first to arrive. Next, several of Lara's friends and relatives show up, along with John's good friends, Misa, Oleg, and Dmitri, with their wives. There is plenty to eat and drink with some music and dancing. Several toasts to the couple are also made during the fun party. Near the end of the party, a small group of guests ask Lara to tell them what they will do on their honeymoon.

"John and I plan on traveling to some of the countries in Europe that I have not been to before. Tomorrow we will fly to Vienna. After a couple of nights in Vienna, we will go by train for one-day visits to Bratislava, Salzburg, and Innsbruck and return to Vienna a different way via Graz. After one-night stays in Graz and Vienna, we will take the train to Warsaw, and after two nights there, we will visit Prague and stay there for several nights. We will then go by train to Chur, Switzerland, to see John's cousin and his family, followed by going to Munich for our flight back to the U.S. I think John and I will continue to live and work in Colorado, and hopefully someday I can get my American citizenship. Of course, we will come back here as often as possible that will hopefully permit John to perfect his Russian."

Later, the guests slowly depart the apartment. After the guests and Vadim leave, Lara's parents escort an elderly friend back to his nearby flat and pick up a wedding gift from him for the Czermaks. John and Lara offer to put the leftovers away and wash the dishes.

Epilogue

After the couple completes putting the leftovers away and washing the dishes, they go into the living room. John is standing in the middle of the room with his back to the entry door. Lara comes over to John and puts her arms around him and gives him a loving kiss.

John says, "I am so lucky to have such a beautiful, intelligent, and fun-to-be-with darling wife."

"John, I am so happy to be your wife and to spend the rest of my life with such a wonderful man."

Lara then sees a man quietly enter the room with a gun, who shouts, "I don't want anyone to take my wife from me!"

She lets out a scream and says, "No, Ivan!" and quickly gives John a bear hug and twists him around so her back is facing the door. At the same time, the man shoots, and the bullet that was intended for John hits Lara in the back. Then the man quickly runs from the room. John frantically lowers Lara to the floor as he calls out for help. While the man is running down the hallway, he passes Lara's folks, almost knocking them down. They recognize their former son-in-law. They hear John's screams and run to the flat to find John trying to stop Lara's bleeding. Lara's father calls the police and tells them to bring an ambulance. A few minutes later, a hysteric John discovers that he is holding a lifeless body.

Acknowledgments

I wish to thank my late wife, Sylvia Tascher, for assisting me telepathically from heaven in my writing of *The Fourth Bear Hug*. Sylvia was a prolific writer, producing two other novels, several books for children, a couple of technical books, and many musical scores and poems.

About the Author

Dr. James D. Navratil was educated as an analytical chemist at the University of Colorado and is now professor emeritus of environmental engineering and earth sciences at Clemson University. His other teaching experiences include serving as a chemical training officer in the U.S. Army Reserve, teaching general chemistry at the University of Colorado, and teaching chemical engineering and extractive metallurgy subjects at the University of New South Wales, Australia, where he also served as head of the Department of Mineral Processing and Extractive Metallurgy. In addition, he was an affiliate professor at Clemson University, the Colorado School of Mines, and the University of Idaho as well as a visiting professor at the Technical University in Prague.

Dr. Navratil's industrial experience was acquired primarily at the U.S. Department of Energy (DOE) Rocky Flats Plant and through his assignments with the International Atomic Energy Agency (IAEA), Chemical Waste Management, DOE's Energy Technology Engineering Center, the Idaho National Engineering and Environmental Laboratory, Rust Federal Services, and Hazen Research, Inc.

Dr. Navratil earned numerous honors, including a Dow Chemical Scholarship, the annual award of the Colorado Section of the American Chemical Society (ACS), Rockwell International Engineer of the Year, two IR-100 awards, and three society fellowships. He was a member of the IAEA team awarded the 2005 Nobel Peace Prize and, in 2006, received the Lifetime Achievement Award for Commitment to the Waste-management, Education and Research Consortium (WERC) and to WERC's International Environmental Design Contests.

Dr. Navratil has four patents to his credit and has given more than 450 presentations, including lectures in more than one hundred countries. He has coedited or coauthored 19 technical books (most recently with Fedor Macasek, *Separations Chemistry*, and with Jiri Hala, *Radioactivity, Ionizing Radiation, and Nuclear Energy*), published more than 250 scientific publications, and served on the editorial boards of over a dozen journals. He was instrumental in the founding of the journals *Solvent Extraction and Ion Exchange* (serving as coeditor for many years) and *Preparative Chromatography* (serving as editor) as well as the ACS's Subdivision of Separation Science and Technology (SST) and its award in SST and DOE's actinide separation conferences and its Glenn Seaborg Award in Actinide Separations. Dr. Navratil has also organized or co-organized many conferences, symposiums, and meetings for the ACS, DOE, and IAEA.

He is a diamond member of the Traveler's Century Club (www.travelerscenturyclub.org), having visited 307 countries and territories on the club list of 327. Some of these travels are described herein.

Summary

The Fourth Bear Hug is a continuation of the stories in *The Bear Hug*, *The Final Bear Hug*, and *The Third Bear Hug*. The story in the latter book begins on the morning following a violent storm. A man and two ladies discover John James Czermak washed up on the shore of Cape Horn, Chile. They take him back by fishing boat to Deborah's home on another island. The couple is Deborah's neighbors, and she is a retired medical doctor. She assists James in recovering but finds out he has amnesia and does not remember anything prior to being washed up on land. Deborah agrees to let him help her around her small farm. Several months later, the two start to travel to different parts of Chile, and a loving relationship develops. James's memory slowly returns after an accidental meeting with a friend in Peru and returns to South Carolina to have a happy reunion with his wife, Ying, family, and friends. Clemson University appoints James as chairman of the Chemistry Department. During this time, Ying gets killed in a hit-and-run accident that was meant for James. A week later, another attempt is made on James's life in his university laboratory, but he manages to escape the Molotov cocktail fire.

James is invited to attend a technical conference in Moscow, and he asks Deborah to accompany him. On the trip, they spend a few days in Vienna, where they get married. The Czermaks then go onto Moscow so James can attend the conference. On the last night of the meeting, the two are confronted in their hotel room by a man with a gun who identifies himself as Nikolai Pushkin, Andrei's son and Alex's elder brother. Before he shoots Deborah and then James, he says, "This is for killing my father and brother." Gravely wounded, James jumps over and gives Nikolai a bear hug, trying to wrestle the gun from him, but it goes off, putting a bullet into Nikolai's heart, killing him.

The story concludes with Deborah dying and James recovering. However, Andrei's brother, Alexei, is determined to kill James since he is convinced that James was responsible for the deaths of his brother and two nephews. However, Alexei is unsuccessful in killing Professor Czermak. John James then returns to work at Clemson University.

The story in *The Fourth Bear Hug* begins after Czermak retires from Clemson, sells his two homes, and moves to Colorado. He then starts working as a part-time professor at the University of Colorado and shares an office with a visiting professor from Moscow. He and Prof. Lara Medvedev start traveling together to meetings, and a loving relationship develops. They attend a conference in Sweden, followed by going to Moscow so John can meet Lara's parents. During this time, Czermak visits a good friend at the Academy of Sciences, where they go to the roof of a tall academy building to take some pictures. Then Alexei shows up and tries to push Czermak off the building, but instead, Alexei falls to his death. Since John now thinks that no one is trying to murder him, he asks Lara to marry him. She happily agrees. A few days later, they have a wedding reception at the home of Lara's parents. The party has a tragic ending.

Globe-trotters should especially enjoy reading about some of the author's travels to various places in the world.